The Lent Jewels

The Lent Jewels

David Hughes

Hutchinson
London

First published in the United Kingdom in 2002 by Hutchinson

1 3 5 7 9 10 8 6 4 2

Copyright © 2002 David Hughes

Hutchinson
The Random House Group Limited
20 Vauxhall Bridge Road, London SW1V 2SA

Random House Australia (Pty) Limited
20 Alfred Street, Milsons Point, Sydney
New South Wales 2061, Australia

Random House New Zealand Limited
18 Poland Road, Glenfield
Auckland 10, New Zealand

Random House (Pty) Limited
Endulini, 5a Jubilee Road
Parktown 2193, South Africa

The Random House Group Limited Reg. No. 954009

www.randomhouse.co.uk

A CIP catalogue record for this book is available
from the British Library

Typeset by SX Composing DTP, Rayleigh, Essex
Printed and bound in Great Britain by
Creative Print and Design Wales, Ebbw Vale

ISBN 0 09 179441 2

For Michael Gough – 'our book'

and in loving memory of

Jill Neville
Tony Brode
George Bull
Jonathan Price
Alan Ross
Martin Shuttleworth

Never disturb the providential strata: take them as they lie: we shall come to the big things in their proper turn.

Archibald Campbell Tait, on office in-trays, to his secretary, son-in-law and biographer, Randall Davidson

Old men should be explorers.

Joseph Haydn

Either the twenty-first century will not exist at all or it will be a holy century. The outcome is up to all of us.

André Malraux

In general terms it may be stated that the tones of an organ are produced by the admission of draughts of air into certain pipes which the player wishes to speak.

John Broadhouse, *The Organ Viewed from Within*

The helpless discomfort familiar to us all in sleep, when we recognise yet cannot reconcile the anomalies and contradictions of a dream.

Wilkie Collins, *The Woman in White*

Part I

One

Almighty God, who hast created man in thine own image, it so happened in April that our Saab had to be serviced at a garage a few miles west of Carlisle. The job would take four hours, so as a courtesy the management dropped me off centrally between a department store and the cathedral, where I would be picked up later.

For this spare time thrown me by chance I had made plans: a pint of bitter at a pub opposite the bookshop, lunch in a restaurant that looked tempting. To hand lay the close – the Deanery sunk in privacy, serene lawns, ruins of a cloister in rose-pink stone – reviving a fear from a sexual event in my boyhood that someone in authority would pop up from nowhere and start asking questions.

What right had I to walk on sacred ground? Who the hell did I think I was?

The scene darkened further within the cathedral. Supervised by a manly lady, a money box the size of a small coffin stood in the way. I had no wish to evade payment, but moral blackmail loomed. Guilt was driving me into the confessional with nothing to confess. I slipped past and drifted off in a light sweat into a vertiginous geometry of transepts, aisles, chapels. The organ towered above the crux of the church, pipes rising into the vault, keyboards hidden: an elephant of an instrument cased in silence. A frisson of the invisible touched me, goose-flesh from the past.

O Christ, who laid aside your glory and lived as a man, what on earth was I doing here? Death was all over the place. Flourishes of gilt inscription glittered off tablets as black as ink. In the cool of the short nave, now a chapel dedicated to the Border Regiment, old battles beflagged the walls. The dead of the last war, name after name, were scripted on to parchment trapped behind panes of glass. The cathedral lofted and narrowed unencompassably. I stared without seeing into vistas of glum stone.

Also glassed in was a flat showcase. It contained bits and pieces like someone's untidy desk, scraps of paper, books scuffed, minute photographs – all of this, in mementoes that looked casual until the weight of their story sank in, all describing the month in 1856, a spring month, when the Dean of Carlisle, Archibald Campbell Tait, and his wife Catharine, suffered the loss, from an epidemic of scarlet fever, of five daughters aged between two and ten.

There in front of me curled the words of record which the Dean had written on the flyleaf of the prayer book he used at their funerals. I glimpsed, not daring to stare at it, a comic sketch he had made of one of the girls to cheer the others during illness; the technique was wispy, the background churchy, the caption 'Be a Good Tait'. Inches above the sketch lay a plaster maquette of Tait enfolded in vestments, a model for his memorial in the cathedral at Canterbury: of which he was apparently to end his career Archbishop.

The collection scared me. It looked like something dreamed, just recollected in time. I had to be nifty in holding on to it or it would escape. It was too flimsy to last. I had to memorise it. In the nag of my mind still hung shreds of outrage at the quantity of the Border Regiment lost in battle. But this small story of a family strongly believing in you, O everlasting God, who hast ordained and constituted the services of angels and men in a wonderful order, struck me as an event hardly less painful to witness than a war killing millions in your son's name, a war which in a parish church of yours pulled down my trousers when I was not much older than the Taits' eldest girl.

The five-year-old Chatty, short for Charlotte, was first to pass over; she died on 6 March.

Her almost two-year-old sister Susan was next to be called home; she died five days later.

Frances breathed her last on 20 March; she died at not quite three years old.

The next, just ten, named after her mother Catharine but called Catty, gave up the ghost on 25 March: the eldest to die.

Her sister May passed on a fortnight later aged nearly nine; she died on 8 April.

Passed on. Gave up the ghost. Breathed her last; called home; passed over. Now we said dead. But these were the terms entombed in the books about them which I later dug up in a library. Only Lucy, an infant born that February, survived, along with Craufurd, a boy of eight. He was also to die early, in his twenties, on the point of taking over his first parish in Notting Hill. In middle age Lucy went on to share with Mrs Benson, wife of the archbishop who was to succeed Tait at Canterbury, the huge bed in which that ample widow had given birth to five neurotics who later made names for themselves, among them A. C. and E. F. Benson. All that too was still six foot deep in the literature.

I gathered now that the girls were buried one by one at short intervals in a mass grave at Stanwix, a village in view of Carlisle across the long bridge over the River Eden. Each of these five deaths sprang from the life-giving privacy of sex between two Christian people who adored each other and God, and were erotic only in the dark when invisible and whose belief was in paradise.

In the cathedral the organ held its silence, a silence almost mocking in tone. I awaited in vain the appearance of a man to play it. O come, Holy Spirit, inflame my heart, set it on fire with love. Yet I wondered if the echo in me of someone's irretrievable loss had anything vaguely to do with having, of all mundane things, to put on the market soon the paradise in the Welsh hills which my wife and I had held on to for twenty years and where our children had been infants.

Two

After poring over the Tait showcase I stood in the north transept and stared at the stained glass dedicated to the memory of the Dean's five daughters. It had the awesome awfulness of much of the nineteenth century's picturing of death disguised as immortality. Archibald Campbell Tait had himself commissioned it. Public subscription had paid for it. It looked as virulent as a bad dream.

Nobody was watching it with me. Whispers carried from unseen parts of the church in shivers down the spine. Perhaps these murmurs arose from tourists, but they sounded like hints of the past. One potent image above me, though small, sharpened the window into vicious focus: a dragon coloured not scarlet but a sickly pink, symbol of the disease that took them off. It pranced amid the no less sickly scenes of innocence and peace that here trapped their childhood in a metaphor of angels and lambs. One of the lambs was practically in the vulpine grasp of the beast, all fangs and slavering tongue, a garish reminder of the symptoms that suffused and distorted the faces of the girls, as they lay gasping.

The predatory creature was off his head; equally he was true to his need: poised in a fever of lust to plunge his teeth into young flesh. The image was of rape, the abuse of a child blazoned across the technicolour face of a window in a building raised to a faith that was supposed nicely to explain the universe. The man in the church of my boyhood stirred in my mind.

I dropped a coin into the box on the way out. The woman at the receipt of custom bowed over my tip with a show of gentility. We eyed each other. Little might she suspect that her modest benefactor was hot on the trail of evil, on the point of burgeoning into a disciple if I emerged from my enquiries unscathed. It had struck me for an instant that I was on the road, if not to Damascus, then to some updated faith – or at least back on that long-lost road, after a lifetime stuck in the ditch or trying to thumb a lift. With a positive spring in my step I walked into the open air amid the rose-tinted ruins of the cloisters.

There was nothing about Archibald Campbell Tait in the bookshop opposite, under either biography or religion. I probably should have gone straight to the Deanery and rung the bell. I envisaged being shown cubbyholes, never cleared by successors, in which the detritus of childhood still lurked. There would be a doll with broken arms. I thought of the piles of old board games packed into a cupboard that no longer shut in our Welsh house, where from birth to about ten our own two children had been mostly brought up. Their heights competed in pencil on a kitchen wall. Their past was stuffed into attics in case they wanted it again, as a spur to memory or a present for their own offspring.

At the pub the pint of beer I suspected Dean Tait would disapprove of my drinking did nothing to slake my thirst for further draughts of his hopeless loss.

A week later I found in the London Library that his

last drink on earth was of wine and water. As usual when browsing in a biography, I had flicked to the last page first, to be in at the death. The book in my hand was quite short, but despite Tait's dying on 3 December 1882, a few hours into Advent Sunday, the date A. C. Bickley's study bore on the title page was that same year. He had plainly merited prompt attention, his fame the spur. As with a newspaper obituary, all but the last few facts must have been set up in type for the book to have been rushed to the shops if not by Christmas then in time for the New Year. Meanwhile the slim volume had not been taken out of the library for four years, so Tait was nowadays an unknown quantity.

At the London Library I had the muffled sense of others searching, on the iron alleys both above and beneath me, in these packed ranks of shelves that shielded everyone's privacy. The occasional clang overhead confirmed a presence, as did the quick retiring footstep of someone who had found what was wanted. Otherwise the silence was so enclosed that the heart of London felt as remote as our retreat in Wales. From the shelves I retired to the reading room, where motionless figures worked, bent in a semblance of prayer, and set down on a desk my small find of books on or by the Tait family.

None belonged to the twentieth century. Tait's chaplain and son-in-law, Randall Davidson, had taken a decade longer than Bickley to produce his biography. He waited until preferment to the Deanery of Windsor offered him leisure to write, and now weightily before me were the two volumes, each of more than 500 pages, which the date stamp told me had been withdrawn only six months ago. This two-decker life of Tait was published by Macmillan in 1891, the year that firm rejected *The Picture of Dorian Gray* on moral grounds.

This time it was not Tait's departure at dead of winter I first consulted, but that early spring when the children died. I was about to plunder the nineteenth century for feelings the twentieth had anaesthetised in me. The list of contents revealed that death had a whole chapter to itself, headed simply 'March and April 1856'. I flipped over the creamy leaves and started to read.

'This chapter must be the shortest in the volume. In vain would any biographer try to describe again the storm which broke upon the Carlisle Deanery in that sad spring. The mother's own hand has given to the world a sacred record which will live in English literature, and which is already known and reverenced in every land. It stands exactly as she wrote it in the very hours of darkness and loneliness which followed upon the storm, and the impress of its birth-time is stamped upon its every page. Not for more than twenty years afterwards – not until she too had passed from earth – was the record seen by any outside the immediate circle of her friends, and the occasion of its ultimate publication was of a piece with the occasion of its birth. To that record, which can neither be abridged nor paraphrased, those must turn who desire to realise what the brightness of the Carlisle home had been, and to know the details of a sorrow, the successive shocks of which were felt, it may almost be said, throughout England.

'Scarlet fever in its most virulent form appeared in Carlisle, and of the six little daughters whose presence had brought radiance to the Deanery, the heart-broken parents were called, within the space of a few weeks, to part with all except the infant who had just been born. One by one, between the 10th of March and the 10th of April, they were laid in the single grave in Stanwix Churchyard. Is it wonderful that when the parents came forth from the awful cloud of those spring days their life was lived thenceforward under wholly new conditions, and that through all the chequered and busy years that followed, whether at Fulham or at Lambeth, they carried consciously upon them the consecration-mark of the holy sorrow they had known?

'The last entry which has been quoted from the [Tait's] diary was dated March 2, 1856. The entry which immediately succeeds it is as follows:

' "Hallsteads, Thursday, 8th May 1856. – I have not had the heart to make any entry in my journal now for above nine weeks. When last I wrote I had six daughters on earth; now I have one, an infant. O God, Thou hast dealt very mysteriously with us. We have been passing through deep waters: our feet were wellnigh gone. But though Thou slay us, yet will we trust in Thee . . . They are gone from us, all but my beloved Craufurd and the babe. Thou hast re-claimed the lent jewels. Yet, O Lord, shall I not thank Thee now? I will thank Thee not only for the children Thou hast left to us, but for those Thou hast re-claimed. I thank Thee for the blessing of the last ten years, and for all the sweet memories of their little lives – memories how fragrant with every blissful, happy thought. I thank Thee for the full assurance that each has gone to the arms of the Good Shepherd, whom each loved according to the capacity of her years. I thank Thee for the bright hopes of a happy reunion, when we shall meet to part no more. O Lord, for Jesus Christ's sake, comfort our desolate hearts. May we be a united family still in heart through the communion of saints – through Jesus Christ our Lord." '

This entry was later to be shaped into a prayer.

I stood in the reading-room window gazing muzzily out. At a diagonal across St James's Square, now smudged by the vast plane trees in the gardens, stood the memory of London House, home of Bishop Tait as he was soon to become. He owed his translation from the northern Deanery in late 1856, at least in part, to Queen Victoria's pitying request to Palmerston that he be offered the diocese of London. The London Library where I stood existed on this site in Tait's time, though in earlier premises. He would need to have belonged. On his way round the square to borrow books he was likely to have glimpsed a contemporary of his, whom I remembered as loitering (perhaps living) in those inner areas where privilege nudged squalor: 'Walter', the self-styled but anonymous Walter, he too represented by words in some dark but enlightened corner of this library; Walter, author of the monumental *My Secret Life*, whose hunt for women was pursued with rare lubricity in the streets close at hand.

Across the square no doubt some outmoded monstrosity of modernism had replaced London House. One of Tait's early acts in that residence, at the time unheard of, was to encourage the nobility, by indulging them in a feast, to face up to the spiritual wants of the London poor: fund-raising. Had the well-born Walter, used to pressing shillings into penurious hands that had just fingered his privates, been present as a guest? Two hundred of the good and the great turned up to the party. One lady, perhaps the rich wife Walter once took and forever regretted, wrote out a blank cheque to write off poverty. In the end more than a million pounds was raised for the benefit of the very people whose daughters Walter was robbing of their virginity in exchange for cash.

So I was within calling distance of the spots where Tait and Catharine his wife installed the remnants of their family, the infant Lucy and Craufurd, the boy of eight, and where Walter haunted the Argyll Rooms with his insatiable lechery. The screen of trees was the blur between me and that reality, the father's feelings hardly shown if ever, the mother's tears shed mostly alone; their joint need to bring others less privileged into the care and mercy of God, while accommodating themselves to the merciless carelessness that seemed to go with the divine plan, while just round the corner in the dark Walter was justifying 'my hope of a heaven, when I have such a taste of paradise on earth as gamahuching and fucking gives me'.

The third book I had found on the Biography L–Z floor seemed promisingly dog-eared. It had the most ancient of London Library labels on the cloth cover; the leather corners were worn by long use. I had guessed what the book consisted of, having seen the footnote in small print at the close of Randall Davidson's brief chapter on the death of the girls. In this volume, taken out a dozen times in the last decade, was contained Mrs Tait's testimony written at the full pitch of her grief.

With it I walked down to the desk, gave my name, showed my card and watched the librarian writing the details out upside down, recording that the flyleaf had come loose, with a note about the sticky tape peeling off the binding, whereupon I signed for it and, for protection clamping it under my arm in a plastic bag, I bore it across St James's Square, averting my eye from whatever had supplanted London House, and at the bus stop in the Haymarket, thinking of Walter's bevy of whores jutting their hips on the opposite pavement in the 1860s where now in the 1990s there was none too posh a cinema, I carried the book upstairs on the 159 bus homewards, left it on my lap unopened down Whitehall and past the House of Lords, where Tait had spoken only when moved to speak, crossed the river holding the book while looking with care into the rooftops of Lambeth Palace, in which Tait had lived for fourteen years as Archbishop of Canterbury, careered round the roundabout with the book almost slipping out of my grasp, the church of St Mary, in whose pulpit Tait had preached, now a garden museum amid the diesel fumes, the bus righting itself where in his time cramped slums crowded round the palace, and with a push on the top-deck bell, book trapped under my arm again, I got off at my stop in the Kennington Road.

Three

When everyone had gone to bed I looked out over the warehouses, a factory in Tait's day but now photographic studios. The Taits lived in Lambeth and so did I. They were only a few hundred yards away, turn left at the lights, skirt a pub or two, sidestep the pigeon droppings under the railway bridge, and you were outside the palace wondering if the nineteenth century still sported a portcullis to keep you out.

The gap actually was hard to bridge. I lived amid the wreckage of their times. World wars and progress had wiped out the slums that girded their palace. I inhabited wastes of bomb damage and shoddy reconstruction that hurt the eye and brutalised the skyline. Walter had vanished too from a district he preyed on. All the lodgings where women lured a livelihood on to their grubby pallets had been crushed out of existence by the building of Waterloo Station during the residence of the Taits. Here south of the river nobody in the past had left anyone in the future much of a place to live in.

I opened the book in the circle of light from the desk lamp. Time had turned the paper sepia. The frontispiece was an engraving of Catharine Tait (thirty-six when her girls died) at the age of fifty. She appeared dressed in dark clothes, if not mourning, her expression rueful, intent, as if listening for something. Her eyes were honest, full of doubt and intelligence. The nose was strong and straight and fleshy, the mouth a bit downturned, wry, hinting at amusement, augustly sensual. Her hair was middle parted with no great accuracy, drawn tightly back behind the ears, under a hat of some dignity tied with a loose bow under her chin. To examine the portrait under a magnifying glass was merely to enlarge the minute stippling of the engraver's craft. I liked her at once.

Facing Catharine was a title-page as staid as a memorial tablet. A page later were half a dozen lines, casual, but crucial to the huge history hiding in the book, signed with Tait's formal initials as Archbishop. Headed 'Stonehouse, St Peter's, Thanet, Jan. 1879' the note read as if just scribbled: 'My dear Benham, – You wish me to send you a letter with some recollections of my wife and son, for the Memoirs which you have kindly undertaken to edit. It soothes my sorrow to comply with your request. – Yours sincerely, A. C. C.'

Catharine Tait's narrative of 1856 occupied 140 pages of the family's book. It was written during the late summer after the spring in which her girls died. The two parents had run from the Deanery flattened by death in the lowlands of Carlisle. Now they were staying among mountains some miles to the south. Friends had lent them a house on Ullswater called Hallsteads, grand enough to be named on the old Ordnance Survey in the 1860s, but unrecorded on our current map. I had to find the spot, however few the remains. It was a place where a woman relived in total honesty the worst that could befall a mother, relived it four more times, and put the quintuple agony on paper with grace and thankfulness: a language I no more knew how to articulate than I did ancient Greek, of which I learnt the rudiments in adolescence but had long forgotten.

Catharine was alone by day. Her husband rode or drove the thirty miles and back to Carlisle to perform his duties, while shutting his eyes to his late home under the cathedral where the germs had invisibly wolfed their brood. She must have seen her words as a necessary record, her debt to her daughters: collision of love and loss that might sharpen her understanding of the unseen; and hopelessly, she hoped, do her good, do good. No doubt she felt it her duty too. As Benham put it: 'A very few days after her first great sorrow had fallen upon her, she committed to writing her recollections of it, for the perusal of her family and a few dear friends. Thus it remained.'

But not for ever. After her death in 1878 they found a note, written four years earlier, in which Catharine Tait expressed herself in favour of publication. 'As the suffering is one which must recur over and over again while the world lasts, it may speak a word of help and comfort to those upon whom a similar burden is laid, and who are feeling that it is too heavy for them to bear.' To which in 1879 her editor William Benham added, 'Private feeling has suggested many doubts as to the publication of these memories of a mother and her son. The request for it came from many personal friends and devout members of the Church. The final decision rested mainly with two persons. The one was Miss [Lucy] Tait, and her judgment was simple and to the point: "If it be thought that the history of my mother's life is likely to do good by helping and encouraging anybody in good living, then let the thing be done, but any other motive ought not to be heard of." ' The other was the Archbishop himself. Much as he shrank from it, he judged on mature consideration that 'the lessons which these Memorials are likely, under God's blessing, to call forth, were too important for the Church of God to allow them to lie buried within the sanctity of home. They comprise a record of deep piety; of an unstinted wealth of effectual sympathy; of untiring labour, along with an exulting love of home, and husband, and children.' I thought of Catharine in her later state at Lambeth Palace looking back on the isolation of Hallsteads, where by the lake's serenity she daily inked in this picture of her daughters under the bare drama of the mountains. Until the Dean cantered back in the dusk she was alone in inexpressible solitude, her flow of words the product of floods of grief.

Again, where was that Hallsteads: did it still exist? It felt as if the nineteenth century had got lost in dream territory. These people were slipping away from me, even as I read about them. To stop reading Catharine was to wake up from something at once forgotten. Calling it back required a concentration that seemed not worth the effort. Let the past stew in what little juice was left, if any. I would never find Hallsteads, or the ethos that troubled that mute lakeside, or the honesty of the woman who in her pain believed in eternal comfort, or the dream they had all passed into.

Yet, Lord of all power and might, who art the author and giver of all good things, the picture Catharine Tait first sketched of her family was one of utter contentment. In October 1855, six months before the first lick of tragedy, the two Tait grown-ups returned from holiday in Ireland with Craufurd, then seven, to meet the five girls who were staying at Allonby on the Solway coast. 'This was our meeting, and I did not part again from our darlings, until we were called by Him who gave them to part with them for ever in this world.'

The parents spent ten days reunited with their children at Allonby 'to enjoy them', to watch them revel in the seaside. When out for a drive the adults would drop the children off in hedged meadows to pick flowers or on safe beaches to collect shells, fetching them home on the trot back, on halcyon afternoons, their baskets spilling over with ripe blackberries. Mrs Tait was five months pregnant with Lucy; here amid her children was a dream of slow leisure, as untimed as dreams, the ideal of all childhood, happiness delineated for good and all. At some point the parents heard the rumour that scarlet fever was rife in Carlisle. 'Still, it was the path of duty, and we felt we ought not to shrink from it,' wrote Catharine fatally.

My vague belief that I was free enough to change my fate, or at least twist its arm, was not shared by Catharine. At any cost − loss of face, loss of income, putting out others, committing any sin − I would keep my children away from the city until the epidemic died out, wouldn't I? But I had an extra century of know-how at my disposal, didn't I? The Taits knew without thinking that life had to go on. I thought without question that life could, must, would, should, be edited by ego or whim or fear.

But my power to alter life rationally was not superior to their quite unreasonable insistence on leaving it to God. Was it or not?

Almighty God, unto whom all hearts be open, all

desires known, and from whom no secrets are hid, the next section of Mrs Tait's memoir was concerned with the family routines at the Deanery. She described each child's participation, according to age, in the daily round.

The four-year-old Frances ('my pretty merry prattler') asking to be forgiven 'all my dear sins', her mother adding, 'she never lived, sweet lamb, to understand what sin was.'

Chatty, just six, (' "my heavenly child," as I used to call her') learning a morning hymn that started 'Saviour, to Thy cottage home', then pointing in her mother's bedroom to a rustic picture she thought must illustrate it: 'She knows more about it now, sweet lamb, than we do.'

By now pain ought to be happening in my present, but it wasn't. There was only the pitter-patter of events sentimentalised by the passage of time. They were not actual because I did not believe them to be actual. I lacked faith in those events. Yet their absence aroused a particular violence in me. I ached to give Catharine a good shaking. 'Let me alone,' I cried into the silence.

Instead I broke off and went to bed. But sleep hardly helped. It took time coming anyway − the fight with this material was even less real than the dreams that broke it up. I was not getting the Taits over to myself; they were still invisible. In whatever way I rehearsed these people, they seemed only dead and gone: as unresurrectible as either pain or happiness.

Four

In the morning I went back to the book, but the exercise was useless even with a hit of coffee. The words were a lot less than words. Sentences failed to cohere, all meaning draining out. Paragraphs were tombstones inscribed with a lost language. I walked away from my room stuffily shelved with death bound in cloth and stomped off into the open.

Round the perimeter of Lambeth Palace – when asked what possessed the young man to walk through Lambeth on his first visit to London, Tait said, 'I wanted to see how I shall like the place when I get there' – nothing modern was in sight. The twin towers squarely bracketing the entry were of early Tudor brick much patched up in later years. The main gates under a Gothic arch were formidable, intended for ceremonial entry by carriage or coach, now shut. The man-sized door at the side also looked beyond breach. Following the wall round the palace amid the roar of traffic, I could scarcely catch sight of a window even by jumping. A heady glimpse of a chapel within made me shudder as my feet jarred back to the pavement. Tait had prayed in that chapel. The high wall sequestered the gardens, except from the top of a bus.

But the nineteenth century was only just in hiding. Any of us now could use half the episcopal garden; Tait had thrown acres open to the public. In this park on the way home I strolled in areas private to the Middle Ages. These rear views of the palace looked more companionable in their mix of styles. Tennis courts, a range of municipal flowerbeds, a football pitch trodden into mud, had taken over from the archbishops.

Moving homewards, delaying a return to the book, I took a glass of bitter up to the open terrace of the Tankard which overlooked the gardens of Bedlam. Here was another London patch of park tamed from the original wild. Here committed lunatics in the 1860s pursued their antics of self-therapy in the open air, while mocked by drinkers in search of gallery entertainment where I now sat. The Bethlehem Hospital had since become the Imperial War Museum. Men temporarily exhibiting their insanity in public had given way to a permanent exhibition of the public insanity of war.

Park-bench drunks were now the only fun to watch as I sat drinking. One, can in hand, wove into a clutch of boys playing cricket, stole the ball squirting lager sky-high at every step, and hurled it at an equally unsteady friend, whose face with a loud crack burst into blood. Children were suddenly everywhere; the boys began running home, their ball the hue of oxblood immobile beneath a tree; a girl in short socks dashed to her father with a screech. Soon, within the minutes it took me to drink up, an ambulance sirened into the park. The injured drunk was lying alone groaning on the exiguous grass. It was time to return to the preferable reality of a book.

I strolled back. The house was empty. At home, in the Deanery at Carlisle, the Tait children were suddenly eager to accompany their parents to the cathedral.

Otherwise they played in the garden or ran in and out of the houses in the familiarity of 'the Abbey', as the close was called.

From mid-morning to dinner time at 1.30 p.m. they were closeted with their governess; taken for a drive or a walk; brought indoors by four o'clock to prepare lessons for the next day, preferring Father's study, lying down without disturbing him – 'dearly did he love the little hum which, like a sweet song, soothed him in his own work.'

After tea, before the parents dined, time was spent with Mrs Tait, the older girls working with tireless charity for the poor, Catty and May stitching a shirt for some disabled pauper with a blind daughter, Craufurd tearing up paper to stuff Chatty's pillowcases; then, infants abed, the others 'crowd round' the Dean to hear him intone Shakespeare. *King John* finished, they were halfway through *Richard II*.

Sundays were 'days of great happiness' with the children singing psalms ('I was glad when they said unto me') in the conjugal bedroom. At family prayers Mrs Tait looked forward to the spring when Catty and May would be old enough to accompany the hymns. Meanwhile these two conducted a Sunday school of all the rest 'up the little steps leading to their father's dressing-room'. Then came 'the longed-for time', ninety minutes of sitting all together outside the Deanery door, reading the *Pilgrim's Progress* in the open air, passers-by gazing 'with pleasure at that happy company'.

Thereafter they joined their father, each in turn climbing on his knee, reciting the hymn or psalm learnt today. The babies were put to bed, followed by more songs and chants until everyone's bedtime, leaving the grown-ups to themselves or each other. All this gathering pace week after short week towards the breathless climax of Christmas.

Through these halcyon days, or rather at night, Catharine and Archie fucked. That was not their word for it, but their neighbour-to-be Walter's. For them the act might be far more intense for being wordless: like prayer. Walter disagreed: he talked dirty and loud; he responded to the whip of urgent words wrenched by his motions from succulent victims, their throats oiled by lust. But in the quiet frontispieces to the books the Taits put on faces to suggest to posterity that persons of their sort never went so far as to fool or kiss or fondle, let alone indulge in foreplay, least of all a fuck.

The quick succession of the babies proved otherwise. Indeed the conception of the first-born, Catty, who was ten when she died, coincided by date with the heat of Florence during the summer which the happy couple spent broadening their minds on Tait's outwardly austere but inwardly desirous version of the Grand Tour. Plagued by insects they wore only the protective clothing of each other's embrace. In bed they were to riot in orgasm as deeply as they later did in grief, rising to the sharpest of both pleasure and pain which the body was heir to. In either case their cries were enough to bring the servants running, with due tact to remake beds drenched in the liquids of life, in sweat or spunk, the blood of birth, lubrication or tears.

But then before the whole agony began there was Christmas! Catty and May were busy making dolls and a cradle as 'a surprise for the little ones', helping their mother choose presents for all, the great anniversary of birth and rebirth drawing close, relatives visiting, and then all of a sudden waking up to that grand dark morning.

The sense of ceremony in 'the exceeding brightness of that home'; dawn prayers indoors, early communion for the adults, the day's 'holy joy' shared in two more services in the cathedral – and then one and all summoned to the study, servants, friends, children (who 'came in in a row, holding by each other's dresses'); the table uncovered to cries of delight, the children carrying round everyone's presents, receiving their own; all five girls receiving dolls from their parents before the choristers swarmed into the drawing room to sing carols for an hour. 'Will the poor old Deanery ever see such bright days again?'

Almighty God, who hast given us thy only-begotten Son to take our nature upon him, all this happiness seemed torture in the light of the shadow soon to fall. Perhaps all human happiness was so fated, letting joy wax only if about to wane: a lunatic platitude. The six months between October and March belonged to a growing family. Each child was changing in perceptible stages, half a year as measureless as a lifetime for a child under ten. The parents too, growing up with their children, growing younger with them, had their weightier burdens lightened by the glow of domesticity unsullied by drudgery. A child unborn uncurled in Catharine's womb: happy, the proximity of a child soon to come into the world. My thoughts swung to Walter, Walter in his thirties, by his own confession impregnating pauper virgins in the London diocese soon to welcome the Taits; God alone knew what happened to those babies born of his spendings. At best they were to slide into the joint abyss of charity and crime.

But the Dean had embraced one grave risk. He took the chance, surely without believing it to be risky, of driving his young family into a hotbed of infection. He had thrown himself on the mercy of his maker. Earlier Tait had prayed deeply before accepting any of the offers or opportunities which had spurred a career so far immaculate: tutor at Balliol, curate of Marsh Baldon, headmaster of Rugby. Prayer, so far, had not let him down.

His calling led him to order his family back to the Deanery when aware of the dangers he was courting. If you trusted in Almighty God, what choice in such conditions did anyone have? How hard to divide your family up between places, when convinced that remaining united was not only proof against any horror the world could unleash, but precisely what God made you for – even if Walter in his lewd solitude believed only that God made you for sex.

Catharine's prose was reaching out towards me, and I had no right to question the truth of her every word, every word that kept itself tautly from weeping. I shrank from the veils of sentiment which her upbringing made her draw over truth; yet what was a turn of phrase but a twist of fashion? I had to shake off my usual impulse to put in the boot of cynicism: a trick of my time, not hers – less a lack of humility than a failure of imagination. I just wished the Dean and Mrs Tait, from wherever their paradise, would slip a sequence of their lives together into my ken, through some medium, if only in a dream.

Five

My next lapse was to forget to take Catharine's evidence with me for company on the train to Wales. Instead I had to read a paperback snatched in a hurry at Paddington – an updated Dorian Gray off the so-called adult shelf, the nearest I could get to Walter in spirit; plus a ready-mixed gin and tonic, a baguette, a quarter-bottle of railway wine – an exciting enough package when hurtling at 70mph into undulating landscape, but not a patch on the eloquent woman I had left behind at home, working herself up to an account of a loss that made losing a house in Wales feel no more than a mild misfortune.

My task was to put our old place formally on the market. The agent surveyed the rooms with a beadily casual eye, measuring them up, taking their measure. I could see the saleable phrases ticking into his mind, while I had spent twenty years wondering how to describe the place. He ignored the immeasurable view, worth a fortune if its value were open to calculation. Meanwhile I looked out on a slowly gathering summer which would end only after I had left the house for good: I knew from his demeanour as he drove off that we were talking more about a quick sale than a slow wait.

His car diminished to silence. I was at a loss. My being here for so short a visit sharpened the impression that I had rarely been here at all. Save in the obvious sense of ownership respected by the solicitors, I had never let the place belong to me, never worked its land or mown its hay or filled its barns, let alone fallen into step with its tradition of upland farmers on their uppers. I opened a bottle. Having a drink on the small lawn that commanded the view, eyeing the sun through the rosy lens of the wine, was to thirst for a state of affairs that had never quite come into being. An ideal sunset illuminated my years of error.

All I had planted here in Wales was a past to which I was now denying myself free access, except in dreams. It was always good for dreams, this house, at dead of night. Into the liquid dark the owls dripped the only sound, apart from the small hours of rain that squalled against the black windows. At such times, a quarter conscious of the place, I dreamed, and knew that I dreamed, and knew further that I dreamed to a purpose; and it was by no means just a dose of therapeutic surreality. These dreams were of a power beyond the personal. They possessed an intent which I kept not quite catching on to when sprung awake in the incalculable solitude of a Welsh night. It was the effect, as they faded, of someone wanting them.

Again wishing to goodness I had brought Catharine Tait's life with me, I went to bed in a silence I was committed to sell, a darkness that was now on the market. Next morning without a backward glance I caught the train to London, having launched this process of loss: selling up a paradise made sense but felt hellish. From outer sun the train slid into the inner shadow of the Severn Tunnel, blotting out a page in the Dorian Gray farce where the painter was about to bend his subject over the easel and sodomise him.

Six

From Paddington I took the tube to Lambeth North, leaving Dorian Gray for someone to sit on or read. At home I ran upstairs and found Catharine on the desk where I had left her.

A daughter had just died, and I had missed it. 'In their own little gardens' the girls were picking flowers to put in the hands of their one dead sister. Mrs Peach the housekeeper fashioned a wreath, and Catharine wrote: 'I said, "It is like her birthday wreath."' To show it off to the other girls Mrs Peach made to put it on the ten-year-old's head.

But Dean Tait pulled her away, 'saying rapidly, "No, not on Catty!" a feeling evidently coming to his heart that to connect his eldest born with death was more than he could bear.'

When Susan, hardly beyond infancy at two, was substituted as a model for the crown, Cousin Nannie said to herself, 'Are they ready to give you up also?'

Then they were taking their last look at Chatty, 'that little form which was that night to be closed from mortal sight.' The wreath on her head, flowers the children had collected in her two hands, Craufurd's offering on her breast. 'We knelt beside that form in agony,' Catharine said, 'for it was hard to part with her;

but strength was given: we felt Whose hand had given, and now had taken her. We know that we shall have her again, though not in this world.'

In what world, though?

Seven

O Lord, you have made us very small, and we bring our years to an end like a tale that is told, but I had spent sixty of them never entering a monastery, even on a visit. Thus it was in a state of ignorance that I was now enquiring into other people's faith. In a state of self-indulgence I was enjoying an infatuation with a long-dead family of believers called the Taits. In a state of grace I was nowhere at all. Some research might improve the perspective. I set off for Quarr Abbey.

This Benedictine foundation in the Isle of Wight was just round the shore from a house where every year we spent a fortnight. I meant to walk the few coastal miles to Quarr as a pilgrim. But the day dawned hot. With a volume of Randall Davidson's biography of Tait on the passenger seat, I drove sweatily, insulated from the everlasting past by ever-present traffic.

Two young monks were working in the walled garden. One wore a lightweight black habit the length of an undergraduate gown. The other was a youth with a thin moustache and a saucer sunhat. The young man was listening to his mentor's wisdom about the wonders of the cauliflower, how it grew, how surprising was its nature. Both looked genially bored with their lot.

The garden was a partial mess. Too many weeds strangled too much food. Courgettes had bulged into marrows that had dried into gourds. But ranks of carrots, celery, cabbages awaited picking for the refectory. Exceptional pears were trained along walls under netting. An orchard sagged under loads of apples. The brethren were unlikely to starve. Around and about the red-brick monastery there was an air of desuetude, well-ordered but impenetrable. The monks had set up a self-perpetuating eternity for themselves.

The chapel was empty, though not void. More silence, gathering layers of it, filled the eardrums to bursting. I forced my patience to donate half an hour to being inside. A visitor or two slipped in and out unseen, evident only because the slightest shuffle was magnified by the acoustics into the echo of a protest march. Every thought had a knack of fading just before caught. Intermittently I reflected on how few resources my mind had, to deal with just sitting motionless for perhaps a very long time before any hint of reward promised a degree of relief.

The only solid doubt that crept into my mind was that if I stayed much longer I would miss my lunch.

On my lap Archie Tait's biography fell open at his childhood. When a schoolboy in Edinburgh he caught, of all diseases, scarlet fever. His elder brother Campbell had suffered during infancy a paralysed foot, which was now cured. He was daily supposed to be off to Portsmouth to train as a sailor. But his journey south was delayed a few weeks to give Archie, focus of the family concern, time to recover for his brother's farewell party.

That night Campbell himself fell ill, of a more malignant strain of scarlet fever. In two days he was dead. Tait was later to say that the shock had affected his whole life. More than ever, as Davidson put it, was he 'thrown in upon himself and his books'.

Not long after, when Archie was ten or twelve, a shaft of light poured into his dark. Throughout his public life he kept this moment quiet. After his death a sheet of folded foolscap was found in his desk at Lambeth Palace. He wrote that in a sermon preached on that day, 22 June 1879, in St Mary's Lambeth, he had dwelt on God's 'revelation to individual souls, rousing them to think of heavenly things', adding: 'The earliest recollection I have of a deep religious impression made on my mind has often since recurred to me with the vividness of having heard a voice from above.'

Tait's note recorded that the event took place in rural Scotland, when as a boy he was visiting a strange house occupied by an unidentified 'old Mrs Rutherford', at the end of a ride on horseback, accompanied by another brother: a trip from the humdrum into the unknown. That night Archie was put to bed in an unfamiliar room, a setting for revelation. 'I distinctly remember in the middle of the night,' Tait wrote, 'awaking with a deep impression on my mind of the reality and nearness of the world unseen, such as, through God's mercy, has never since left me.'

The reality and nearness of the world unseen.

That night was embedded for ever in the blanket silence that hardly warmed the nineteenth century against the chills of doubt. As a boy Tait was living in a climate of belief in which the mind was readier to recognise, perhaps keener on wanting, any old road to Damascus. On the verge of puberty, from horror of the body's eruption into the start of manhood, Archie might well have been ready to be blitzed by faith. That night, exiled from home, his apprehension of being in an unknown world meant that he was close to an unknowable one. That night he may have had a peculiarly vivid dream; perhaps this sense of meaning that came over him, overcame him, was glimpsing what seemed truth, askance in the awkward angle of a dream not efficiently remembered.

On the same private sheet of foolscap in 1879 the Archbishop continued: 'I have fallen into many sins of omission and commission; I have had many evil desires, and have gratified them; but this sense of the reality of the world unseen has remained with me through God's mercy. What the value of the impression was it was difficult to say, but that it was made by God the Holy Ghost working on my soul I have no doubt.' Understanding took a stumble here: my own cast of mind, or historical time, distanced me from his.

Why did sins of omission take precedence over those he committed?

Were the desires against which he put up no fight as evil as those flaunted on Walter's every page?

And what did Tait mean by 'the value'? He seemed to give a new value to this word, in other words an old one.

In the chapel I stopped reading or, rather, woke up sharply, neck cricked, book on floor. Nobody was occupying any of the confessionals. You had only to apply to the porter and help would be instantly summoned. What the devil would Tait confess? For my part I was not close enough to faith for any confession to have any point. I lacked belief in having committed any sin serious enough to be hissed through the grille. No religion had numinous rights over my guilt. If for some people these booths led to peace of mind, to me they were closets for the morally incontinent.

I stepped into the fresh air, still afraid of missing lunch. Down a rough lane, yards east of the abbey, stood the craggy gate to the original monastery founded in the fourteenth century. Irregular stonework petered out into fields.

Within lay a working farm founded on monastic ruins. Was it still holy ground? Crumbles of medieval cement held up the tracery of a rose window in a pasture steaming with cows. A hay-stuffed barn had once been the refectory. The decrepitude of history was there for anyone to mourn or to revel in. Grey lengths of wall that had once contained meditation now meandered, half-wrecked, across acres of site.

Here at Quarr Abbey they would let me stay for a spell. I could be the guest of silence. What stopped me believing that retreat in a monastery must lead, if not to faith, at least to comprehension? Things existed to be gone beyond. I simply had to muster the rigour to manage an advance on my own terms. I must not fall into the hands of the ready-made or the ritual.

I dreaded total solitude draining me. Faith must be able to emerge from the rough and tumble of the way I normally lived. And then survive it.

Did I not have a god-given right to faith?

I emerged from these scraps of past into the Isle of Wight's own brand of bedlam: a bank holiday rally of highly accoutred scooters, studded from handlebar to mudguard with dozens of rear-view mirrors, blinding the motorists stuck in jams behind the splutter of their ins and outs down Ryde's Union Street; then a siren, and a second siren, distant but blaring nearer, a pair of fire engines in full career, forcing me to swerve, heat beating down from the sunroof; and by the pier lolled men in fat jeans drinking out of cans, and out of big mouths abusing becalmed drivers as the fire brigade stormed past. I thought of the missed opportunity to confess all, in one of those mute booths, to confess my hatred of my kind, to deny my commitment to things material, to utter my shame at not being stronger in my embrace of the unseen and unknown.

The puzzle of the monastery remained. It lacked any trace of the vision which Tait had murmured of seeing. On the Isle of Wight the traffic was hell until I turned into our place by the beach. We ate and drank in the sun. The moment felt like permanence. Across a glimmer of calm water stood Chichester Cathedral in the mainland haze, the spire luminous in our telescope: a magnification of my first entry at the age of nine into a church, a cathedral, the Church of England, in the first month of the last war, to the welcome of an organ at full blast.

Eight

On the afternoon of 3 September 1939, evacuated by the chance of train timetables to Chichester, we children were shown the film of *The Invisible Man* to keep us in the dark and out of mischief, while the authorities found billets for us. We were aged nine or ten, girls and boys. In the first days of missing my home in a London suburb through fears of a German attack, in a stranger's house somewhere out in the hostility of the countryside, I was dogged by the invisible man. My eyes detected him everywhere. He was larger than life because nobody could see him.

The outside of my billet – lawn large, trees high, sky huge – slipped into dusk and throbbed with quiet. For a child it was full of whatever mystery London lacked; it presaged Wales and my own children. Upstairs the maid bathed me with hands that slid down my soapy body and ruffled my hair, and her blue eyes brimmed at me. She tucked me into the luscious mattress against pillows that soused my head in silence.

I had never heard such silence as when the maid left me to myself. The night outside was beyond infinity. A faint light blinked through an inch of door into the passage and I saw with a shudder the invisible man enter the room.

The man was here and now. Shaping him in the air, the curtains hung in drowsy folds, stirred by a slightly open window. The man moved about his unknowable business, declining to reveal a glimpse of his identity, and I would never sleep again – until abruptly the curtains were whirred aside, the morning light blinded me, and the maid was there, with a cup of tea in her normal hand and on her head the blank of her starched cap.

These opening phases of war in Chichester were tied up with the cathedral I dared not enter. It was a haunt of invisible men. As years later at Carlisle, in the ache for something in excess of myself, I was drawn by magnetic fright to the very composure of the cathedral close. Only spectres seemed to be living in its quiet houses, vanishing figures in black turning corners even as I looked. I was caught by the vista from the Residentiary's front door, confidently left half open, through several white-panelled rooms in furnished shadow, to another open door beyond which a mown perspective of lawn could be glimpsed. I saw then that for much of the time all rooms were empty, unoccupied but looking preoccupied, as was a cathedral, that most gigantic of rooms, as perhaps were many people half the time. There was nobody in us.

The cathedral! When first brought to that mute and deafening chamber I had no idea what was to happen within. I knew merely that we – my father, a dark young man and I – were entering at dusk by a side door reached through a cloister when nobody else was visible or present. In single file, our steps an affront to the silence, we walked through shifts of perspective unlike anything I had seen or even suspected, and against all likelihood started up a spiral stairway, as if to heaven, our shoes now clanging an echo that made the extremity of the roof seem miles off.

After a giddying ascent, in due order after the organist and then my father, I came out on to a platform that seemed to occupy the midway air between these cliffs of stone. Here all was gloom, until suddenly the click of a switch revealed a panoply of ivories, four keyboards, dozens of stops, circlets of blinding white inscribed with a foreign language in letters of black, all clues to the mystery I was about to be introduced to, as I felt the immense weight of the building hammering in my ears.

After producing light at a touch, the organist pressed the button that conjured up the wind. It swelled into the bellows, a sigh of air entered the church, a just audible ghost rising: I felt in the presence not of a machine, but of someone breathing.

An exchange of courtesies, which I only just grasped, took place. The organist, with an impresario's wave of the hand, deferred to my father, who was flexing his fingers. All smiles, they shrugged and gestured: one adult dying to show off his pet, the other longing to put a giant through its paces. I waited with not the palest idea of what might eventually emerge either from the dispute or the instrument. Then the organist swung his legs over the stool – and all was settled. My father and I melted into shadow.

The briefest of intervals allowed the organist to pull out his pick of stops. For a moment he let his fingers dally in the air over the middle manuals. Then his hands dropped: an almighty pause; and from the heavens above my head sprang such a burst of sound that no notes were distinguishable in it, a noise huger than sound, with the impact of light breaking in through the vault.

I reeled back from the tremendous chord, buttocks tightening, feeling swelling into my throat. For a long instant the chord held, packing the church to the doors with harmony that cheered itself to the echo; and then more softly, sidling into the lessening echo, high above and far away, a tune began, and this tune persisted, and lower down in the scale the same tune entered, and mingled with the first notes in a fruitier voice, whereupon that very same tune slipped in higher up the scale and reedily elongated itself, and in a minute this now familiar and growing melody growled at a richer depth as the organist plied the pedals, until my ears were awash with a grand progress that twisted on and on down corridors that thickened into mazes that arrived after many a complexity at the triumph of a solution.

The organist had played what I later knew to be a fugue. My ears were deafened when I was nine years old by a belief in the awesome and the absolute with my father holding my hand. I was all too ready to be packed from top to toe with faith. How I longed sixty years later to be feeling a vestige of that faith, know what lay beneath it and sense what lay beyond, and understand Catharine.

Nine

Blessed Lord, who wast tempted in all things like as we are, I put off, because here on holiday by the sea, reading more of the document written by Catharine at Hallsteads after her girls died. I skimmed bits, then pushed it aside, scared of facing a reality that accorded not at all with my experience, also wanting not to spoil these days in the sun that were as fragile as those the Taits spent at Allonby that summer a century and a half ago.

It would help to be at the very spot where the thirty-five-year-old Catharine committed her grief to the page, even if nothing were left of Hallsteads to see or of her presence to sense. Too easily, in today's heat, she faded into the unseeable woman, companion to the invisible man who had appeared, or failed to appear, on and off through my boyhood.

At night she was in my room, coffined in the volume on the bedside table if I lay awake, but wandering the spaces when I nodded off. Her tragedy was still a closed book, her unique view of it a map I had yet to find a way of reading. As I fell asleep, my feelings for Catharine paralleled the feelings I had for dreams, which every night perturbed me with their want of explanation. For years I hardly dared to entertain an intuition I had long ago of their purpose. But now, again, what dreams intended, where they went, seemed at the moment of shutting my eyes less lost than close. By morning I had forgotten.

I tried the book again early next day, with a sense that I had heard it all before and missed it. Others in the family were devouring scrambled eggs and newspapers, when I hit upon the Taits at a good moment just before the first daughter died. 'On Monday dear Chatty and Susan were on my bed together at breakfast,' Catharine said, 'full of fun as I played with them; but, as Chatty was lifted off to go out, I said to her nurse I thought her pale . . . A pleased and most sweet look of love lighted up the face of each. I watched them for a few minutes, and said to some one who was near me, "Did any one ever see two such sisters?" and a vision of brightness never to be realised came over me, of life going on with these most sweet daughters, for every one of whom seemed to open a field of unusual promise. It has opened in brightness indeed, but they are hidden for a season from our eyes.'

In the background my teenage daughter, drawn by the scent of coffee, ghosted out of a bunk bedroom. She had been up until the small hours carousing on dark beaches at the ebb tide. 'Good morning, darling . . .' Her eyes dipped and she slumped. The book drew me back.

'She continued a little poorly all day, and at four in the afternoon, when I went to the drawing-room . . . she looked little, and seemed weak and hot, also a look about her eyes gave me a feeling of anxiety . . . She seemed very languid, as if she could not bear noise. I put her on the sofa, and she went to sleep. When she awoke I took her in my arms; she was very hot, and seemed quite poorly. I sent for Mrs Peach, and said she should not return to the nursery. (Ah! sweet lamb, you had seen your nursery for the last time.) We agreed that a little bed should be made by the side of my bed . . . I went to bed at ten, but could not sleep; why, I know not. Their Father, who had been dining out, came to see me and to pray with me before he left me. We neither of us felt uneasy about our Chatty. Yet a sadness seemed resting upon me . . . Once or twice in the night I heard her say "Where? where?" as if angels told her of a brighter home ready for her. Towards morning, but still in a deep sleep, she raised herself in her little bed, and in a voice which told its tale to my poor heart, she said the following prayer, her usual prayer for night: "O my God, teach me to love Thee. O my God, teach me to pray. O my God, keep me from sin. Pray God to bless me, make me a good and holy child, and keep me to Thy heavenly kingdom. Forgive me all my sin. Teach me to know and love my Saviour Jesus Christ, who, when on earth, suffered little children to come unto Him, and whose child I was made at my baptism. Bless my dear father and mother, my dear brother Craufurd, and my sisters. Bless my dear little baby, for Jesus Christ's sake. Amen. Our Father," etc . . .

'I felt much alarmed, and a weight of sorrow came on my heart; it was the first time that a sense of danger for any of my children came over me. I heard her Father come into his dressing-room, and rapped for him to come to me. He came at once, and was much distressed and astonished to find me crying . . .'

A flush from the lavatory disturbed the quiet of our seaside house. From a pure sky the sun poured down on the Solent that looked as tranquil as a lake. Hallsteads felt close. The morning was already hotting up. On the page a day and a night had passed.

'I little thought that in a few hours after I was to kneel to give her up to that dear Saviour for ever; but so it was. She seemed tired when she had finished her prayer, and lay back to rest, but when her breakfast came she sat up and seemed to enjoy it . . . She lay quiet for a few minutes and and then sat up and began to look at the pictures she was so fond of, and soon after, looking at me in a strange, wild manner, began to open her mouth in a fearful way . . .'

O my God, teach me to love Thee. She was five years old. Where, where, did I, or you, or anyone else, go from here, O God, who art the author of peace, and lover of concord, in knowledge of whom standeth our eternal life, whose service is perfect freedom? Etc.

And et cetera. At the end of the holiday, on the car ferry from Fishbourne backing towards the mainland, our daughter's frown directed at the churning of the sea in the glitter, our son's gaze loitering over electronic games in the saloon, both having grown to their own points of reference, which meant detachment from Wales and so from me and so from loss, and I realised that time numbed but did not heal: time being an anaesthetic applied to the incurable.

As we stole into harbour the children gathered back into domestic harmony and the four of us drove ashore together in a car quartered by loneliness and united by love.

Part II

One

O Lord, who has taught us that to gain the whole world and lose our souls is great folly, I had intended all day to turn up at the launch of a friend's book. A buffet was promised; I would see chums. I had a slow bath, put on my grey suit brightened by a tie to celebrate, and walked out into the Kennington Road to miss a 159 bus by a whisker.

The weather was heavy, the pavement damp from recent drizzle, no bus reared into sight down the infernal length of our plane-lined street. I thought about the silence I had left behind in the house, a silence to be unbroken until my return. It was there to plunder now – and my mind muttered: break back inside the house and try praying; or try at least burgling the idea of prayer, with no party junketing in your ears.

I ran across the road between traffic and let myself back in. The house stood still. By closing both door and window I corklined this room against outer noise. It all looked as if I should not be here at all. It was my turn to be the invisible man. I had come back to corner an imponderable. I felt better than I had in days.

At the desk many things I loved in theory surrounded me in symbols. They made no pattern: snaps of my parents in oval frames, reference books that held what my brains had too little room for, a wooden owl, an ammonite dug out of the cliff at Bonchurch in the

47

1960s, Beethoven quartets on tape, an ashtray my son made at primary school, a drawing of me at work by my daughter. They made no entity. If I were to worship myself, no doubt memory could gather these objects into a passable myth.

Opposite my workroom window cameras flashed from chinks in the black curtains of the studios. In the warehouse updated from Tait's time they were busy fixing for eternity the transience of chic. Meanwhile photography was also blinding guests into immortality at the party where I ought now to be.

As a choirboy I had knelt in prayer and winked at the fellow in the stall opposite. I had not knelt at a bedside for years, though it was once taught me by my father as a way of ensuring sleep. I wanted not at all to sleep, except perhaps with the elusive Catharine caught in my arms. This was fantasy: the plump dead luxury of Catharine. I recognised it as part of an infernally tangled wavelength of wishful thinking and memory. The stuff dreams were supposed to be made on. Surely dreams were only evidence of the nocturnal psyche helping people through the trials of daylight? Long ago I had become a spy, first, a spy on reality, trying to pick in advance those aspects of the actual which would be transformed into dream. I had been pursuing them in all their flighty significance for half a century, while at the same time I had wondered where faith was actually to be located, then pinned down. On the odd occasion I had recounted them to a battery of yawns round the breakfast table. The family reminded me that the only place for a dream bore was on the consulting-room couch: Freud's expense of money on a waste of time.

Here in my Kennington room I thought of the war

deepening into the winter of 1943 in Hampshire. We choirboys were practising carols in the organ recess curtained off from the cold church by swathes of baize on brass rings. The shrill cheer of the carols had softened the sub-organist's normally sullen disposition. A man of few words, he touched the off switch. The wind died away within. Flexing his knuckles, he pointed at a hidden door in panelling to the side of the console. One hand gripped a torch. The beam focused on a keyhole.

'I'll take one or two of you up,' he said, 'into things beyond your ken.'

It was the moment I had unwittingly awaited since that outburst of the mystery of sound in the dark in Chichester Cathedral three years earlier, when the fugue soared into the roof of my mind and the invisible man was at my back.

Light wobbling, key met keyhole with an oily suck. My gut raced. Here was to be an ascent into a supreme secret.

The sub-organist creaked open the door. He bent his bald head under the low lintel. His trousers appeared to levitate. Inside rose a set of narrow stairs. I gaped upward, legs weak. 'Only one boy at a time,' said the sub-organist. The worn soles of his shoes receded into the gloom. The torch snapped on above. A globule of light whizzed out of control as the man tripped and cursed, then cast down an unsteady beam on the steps. I followed the lure.

Cramped footways seemed to be linked by ladders at several levels. Within seconds my head was close to a rise of tiny pipes that lifted out of the torchlight. My head moved up another few feet, and I looked down on a range of square wooden pipes with stoppers on top. I could almost hear the scale as my eye followed their ripple upwards.

Panting with effort or elation, I paused alone in the midst of serried ranks of tin or wood, trying to take stock, in blank wonder. This great interior seemed poised for a great event – an event which a boy by himself could launch. I wanted to know how to play. It was that simple. Somewhere in the dark the sub-organist was glumly humming an unrecognisable tune. Sidling up and down the strait ways between such foreign countries as lieblich gedacht, corno di bassetto, hautbois, diapason, I breathed dust. It wafted centuries back to my nose. I knew I was surrounded by unspeaking harmony.

I came down the ladder shaking. I longed at once to go back up again. The choirmaster's shoes were almost stamping on my fingers. He switched off the torch. The key crunched out of the lock. A whole language was shut away in the dark. The boys followed his footsteps across the invisible void of the church into the blacked-out street.

At the function I had missed in London goodbyes were now being uttered by people unsteady in thought and limb. The party was over. I now knew what I most feared in this game called living in the present. I feared nothing happening, no change, no progress. So I wanted nobody else involved, until I had envisaged for myself a form of faith that was not a formula.

At my desk I closed my eyes to blot out the familiar associations – paperknife, fossil, owl, matches, watch – and swimming into my ken, with no clarity, came the first whispers of children I could believe in, the Tait children, because they were just like ours had once been in Wales, and at this last minute, in the shudder of loss I had craved all evening, I sank to my knees and wept and thought myself a child.

Then to my relief I heard a key in the front door and a shout of hello.

Two

In the chase for revelation, almighty and everlasting God, who alone workest great marvels, I was attending mass at St John the Divine in Kennington, our local church. The marvel of recalling the interior of that organ in Hampshire's dark of long ago was still upon me, as was 'the reality and nearness of the world unseen', young Archie's apparition of divinity even longer off. But how to enter it? Through some experience of mine embedded in memory? Praying here in church, even pretending to pray, gave the mind plenty of room to roam. It freed me of time.

Several memories hinted at revelation or passed for it. First came waking in the night at an old house in Hampshire (in my thirties) to hear curtains being drawn in another room where nobody was; or one hot afternoon (repeated on other summer days) the noise of a barrow being wheeled on gravel where now there was only grass: if a world unseen, a world very near.

Then lying in bed as a boy (under eight) in Normandy Street, Alton, Hants, hypnotised by the dying sun on the bare scarlet brick wall of the house next door, unsleepy, but with a sleepy ignorance of what was going on within our house, feeling secure in its worth: an elementary lesson in the world unseen, but safe; unknown, but merciful.

Then being awoken (at aged twelve) to see in 1942 a

scatter of incendiary bombs candling the black hillsides beyond the bathroom window, a domestic image of war that remained on the inner retina after more than half a century: a threat that was also a dream, an invisible enemy who like a god was lightening our darkness.

And being ensconced in bed at home in Wales (at sixty-eight) listening to the weather outside, gaining from its hostility the warmth of being privately alive: brain and the spirit joining forces, each mistaking the other's identity, but in snug cahoots; rain and wind emphasising – now that we were putting up the property for sale – the imminent loss of the darkness where I lay.

And taking a modest dose of LSD in the mid-seventies, stark naked to be open to any freedom the drug might offer, one afternoon with a lover in Chalk Farm when time and space cut out, being determined to tape-record words to explain it but sliding quickly beyond words, and finding my ego paranoid in the extreme and my body charged to the extent of seemingly endless orgasm: sex our only god, all that was left, in earthly life at least, of an ecstasy beyond reason.

Or being struck by an excess of well-being (at thirty-seven) in a restaurant under awnings on the Carlton beach at Cannes in the shaded but blazing space between mornings of watching films at the festival and afternoons also spent in the half-dark, gazing in exhilaration into the super-bright twinkle of the Domaine Ott blanc de blancs twirled in my fingers against the sun, while swallowing the ocean of an oyster: the sensual, for a second, nudging the spiritual.

And looking amazed at my vanished youth in a Greek copy of the *Antigone* picked up off the shelf under S for

Sophocles, while waiting to hear what the classics master thought of my son's performance in that tongue, and understanding not a word of either the play's language or its foreign world, both of which as a boy I knew well. The sense of having totally lost a secret, which once in youth I had nearly caught, drenched me with a conviction that secrets did exist somewhere, like dreams, and could yet be plumbed.

I opened my eyes in church. On review, the above was a pathetic catalogue of experiences that approximated to revelation, even if, pursued, they might have led to it. Each was an isolated whack in the bowels of my assumptions. They neither added up to a philosophy nor cohered into a faith. They were footnotes to a lifetime of wishful thinking. But one I had forgotten, though I had noted it only days ago; my mind had just to touch the edge of it to start back in shock.

It sprang from suddenly thinking in Montpelier Street (when forty-five) of the proximity at night of other sleeping minds, bodies in a packed town at odd angles to one another in beds and at differing levels, and thus of the possible interaction of dreams down a whole terrace, along the mews opposite, up in the square: generating a contact as invisible as electricity throughout a city.

The idea swilled through my mind in a flood of hesitant understanding. This, for heaven's sake, might sweep away all the sad efforts I and my generation had made to come to terms with, or fall headlong into, or with hysteria deny, extrasensory perception. It could cancel out for good the games of guessing in padded cells what numbers people had written down on folded scraps of paper or what animals they had sketched behind closed doors. In other words my sudden revelation voided the brain of paranormal rubbish – and left it wide open to an illusion far grander. That we did not just share dreams (that now seemed trivial) but created them for onward transmission.

For, living in Montpelier Street, going to bed in an auburn glow of street lamp with a pub sign lit opposite, making love in this light with a fervour that Walter himself might jealously admire, it came to me one night, as her haunches shifted over me yet again in a doze of the lascivious, that no longer was I forgetting dreams in the normal way – I was having them stolen. They did not slip my mind. I was being inwardly burgled.

At once I felt that no other bundle of brain cells in human history had been brave enough, or had had the effrontery, to come up with this particular plain answer to any number of questions; and though I could in no way prove it – give me time, give me luck – I sensed it to be true. True in its own way. Not exclusively true, of course. But a good working faith, a faith to play havoc with the paltriness of most belief, a faith to knock much world religion into a cocked hat. Here was what people in Kennington, London, England, Europe, the World, the Universe, were aching to hear. This world of collected dreams was the world unseen.

Had any such moments of vision ever struck me in church, as now, during a service – at a solemn moment – the vicar raising the chalice on high, a murmur of the old words, O Lord, who hast taught us that all our doings without love are nothing worth, words that tolled halfway between heart and mind, satisfying neither? Since Archibald Campbell Tait officiated at such services in the musty nobility of the language of 1662, the words had lost their nerve by being modernised, just as I seemed to have lost my nerve by pretending to be modern. Now I just had to find language that had the knack of the eternal.

Three

Next morning for relief I set off in search of Walter. On the top of the 159 bus I thought that it might be easier to identify with this contemporary of Tait: faithless, unbelieving; a chap more likely to jump the gap between then and now; a fellow subject to ordinary if exaggerated appetites; a man unconcerned with salvation. Walter's dates were right. Born nine or ten years after Archie, roughly the same age as Queen Victoria, Walter from boyhood enjoyed circumstances so little different from Tait's in class and affluence that they might have been friends: chatting about their conquests, whether of tarts or of sins.

They were spheres apart, though. While Tait occupied the middle years of Victoria's reign with an increasing influence over affairs of the spirit, apart from a sex life that produced nine children in fourteen years, Walter was captivated purely by sex for its own sake, apparently producing no children in wedlock but unwanted ones from maidservants. He felt a lack of guilt as unlimited as Tait's sense of guilt was limitless.

Walter's days were spent writing, and his nights collecting material for, an erotic tome of biblical length. Few cognoscenti of filth believed it ought to be, like the Gideon Bible in hotels, in everybody's bedroom at home. It was ruder than Genesis and more repetitive than Numbers. The dubious Walter was as wholly private in public as the doubting Tait was utterly holy in public and dogged by anxiety in private. Each for different reasons was haunted by the fear that he would be found out, Archie for putting worldly ambition before purity of soul in the sight of God, Walter for exploiting every chance to seduce any woman in sight. Each faced the police of the unknown. One eye on his God, Archie felt his way into the recesses of his own mind. One eye on the guard, Walter felt his way into young widows on the South-Western railway. Both might be esteemed as men who with dedication pursued their overheated ideals to the last gasp but who were, in short, fantasists.

On my way to Hatchards to see whether they stocked *My Secret Life*, as I wandered up the Haymarket, the idea for an instant gripped my mind that Archie and Walter were one and the same man. (Or had I just begun to feel equally at home with both?) A bishop after dark, disguised by the very murk of his apparel, had the freedom of movement on which Walter fed. His calling was a passport to leave home without excuse on expeditions unnecessary to explain. London's midden was on his doorstep. The black streets flared by gaslamps disguised him in their shadows. An invisible man hunched in an ankle-length overcoat – of the kind Walter often flapped open to cast to a minor the fat bait of his tumescence – the bishop slipped out at night.

Returning in the small hours from his encounters with 'fallen women', as his friend Gladstone put it, he sat at his teak desk while others slept, writing out at speed his sermons on sex, his athletic gospels of the miracles of potency he was performing, to spring up at daybreak fresh for family prayers in the presence of the very servants he had now and then bent forward over occasional tables or had kneeling on the carpet: a man as devoted to the body as to the spirit. What a perfect shit, what a god among men!

Now gazing into the present squalors of Great Windmill Street, crammed to the doors with absence of style, I decided with reluctance that I had no case in allying the bishop with the lecher, at least not literally. But I knew the men might well have met. In 1859 both had no doubt cast their glance on Gladstone's 'no common specimen of womanhood', whom the Prime Minister was luring off the streets with liberal doses of Tennyson and other poetical redeemers heavily breathed into her ear.

Walter was rich enough at times to fall a prey to charity, if only to clear his conscience, if he had one, as indeed he claimed. In the book he kept his social status tightly to himself, unlike his private parts. But between the lines, otherwise busy with cheaply bought orgasms, I gathered from modern commentary on his work that as a gentleman he was certainly entitled to be received at London House by the Taits. A few yards from an alley where he had just touched up a slut, he would be fawned upon, announced, ushered into episcopal saloons, for the purpose of being fleeced. He would enjoy to the full the huge and classy crowd, as hyper-critical as hypocritical, who attended only to be seen, and be seen to write cheques. He might thus relish more sharply the irony of paying up his whack for the poor, in particular the female poor he was already supporting for services rendered. He favoured coffee shops that had indiscreet beds advertised with dis-cretion in the window. He liked such chambers to be equipped with a cheval glass and to have a spyhole into the next bedroom.

If none of this, Archie and Walter by the laws of coincidence passed each other somewhere in St James's on the way to the same or a similar club. They doffed hats in the mistaken impression that they recognised each other. They walked on with due puzzlement. London was even then a small town, gutters stinkingly close to smart drawing rooms. Tait could not have been unaware, as he stepped abroad, of unholy pleasures brushing his shoulder or stirring his mind. Their noise swelled his nights. Inflammations of desire passed his very door. Women squatted to piss in courts as he trotted past, on the way home in a dark hansom from a state function, to confront his own tragedy close to, or locked away from, his wife Catharine. Meanwhile in 1859, three years after the deaths of Tait's girls, his friend Gladstone wrote 'full in the highest degree of both interest and beauty' of the latest prostitute he was whipping himself up to rescue.

'Walter' was alas 'out of stock' at Hatchards. On the other hand the shelves properly groaned with bibles.

Four

Someone tipped me off that the library at Lambeth Palace possessed a Tait collection of letters, books, diaries. So much of the man existed in permanent form so close to home in Kennington. The palace looked as fortified against research as its past was against attack. But one phone call, briskly answered, and I got my orders. A publisher's letter of recommendation, two passport photos of myself, municipal proof of residence, these would grant me a reader's ticket for five years. Within a day I had assembled this material. I dropped the envelope through the Archbishop's front gate, above which a portcullis had clearly once hung.

In pursuit of Catharine, while I waited, I came across a house closer to home which she had made her own. Cornered by blots of suburb on the Ordnance Survey lay the outline of Addington Palace. A mile or two east of Croydon, the house had served as the country seat of nineteenth-century archbishops. Five primates were buried in the churchyard, as were Tait's wife and only son. Tait himself chose later to lie between them. These dolorous arrangements were made in advance at the family's request. A spot in Surrey – 'this quiet village is a great delight,' Tait said – must have struck them all as paradise or at least its ante-room.

One of the surviving daughters, Edith, born after her five sisters died in 1856, married the man from whose fluent prose I was tapping this information. Having once been his chaplain, Randall Davidson followed in his father-in-law's footsteps as primate. Davidson died aged eight-two two months before I was born in 1930. His two-volume life of Tait was 'a masterly piece of work', according to G. K. A. Bell, Bishop of Chichester in 1940 when the sounds of that almighty organ in the cathedral first burst on my ears; in 1914 he was domestic chaplain to Randall Davidson during the latter's prelacy. As a boy I half saw Bell flitting about the close from a canon's lawn of ghosts to his own palatial secrecy. A city like Chichester was a tiny world in which friendship composed the politics. Devotion was taken as read, while books were written.

Still postponing the emotional bewilderment I feared from affinity with the mother of the five girls, I kept ingesting these male facts – ambitions, promotions, vocations – to delay reading Catharine in full. Why, why? I had to make myself good enough for it all, that was what, or put myself in a good enough mood to suffer it.

I looked up Addington Palace. In 1971, the first publication date of Pevsner's *Surrey* in 'The Buildings of England', the house was occupied by the Royal School of Church Music, founded by a queer old dear called Sir Sydney Nicholson. Round my neck in 1943 as head chorister of our parish church in Hampshire, I wore a medal hung on a blue ribbon. This proved that the choir's existence and mine were approved by Sir Sydney. I fingered it with jittery pride when I sang a solo. On his rounds he had once visited our town to judge the harmony of our performance. I recalled a glimpse of trim beard wagging under a thin smile. He died in 1947 three years after my voice broke.

The palace, I now learnt, was built of Portland stone over six years from 1773 for Barlow Trecothick, Lord Mayor of London. The garden was planted with swanky cedars. The archiepiscopal retreat had gone secular in 1897, fifteen years after Tait's death, bought by a South African diamond merchant. He paid Norman Shaw to enrich the austerity of the interior. A golf links had smoothed the former gardens, where Mrs Tait used to grow the masses of fruit and greens she gave to the poor in hampers. I trusted a living place to resurrect a dead person.

Next morning, along with the map, I took Catharine Tait's testimony, as a talisman rather than a guidebook. A day of full sunlight showed up the brick of south London as a waste of space in a desert of time. In a carriage from Lambeth Palace, after negotiating at a trot a few downtrodden lanes of pimps and pickpockets, Archbishop Tait on the canter to Croydon had the roll of the Surrey hills to uplift his spirit. Today's spirit was raised by nothing in sight. Today's hills were topped by a crust of suburb.

Driven fast down the shallow abyss of the Brixton Road, the bus shook out a jumble of phrases from the book. I tried to hold it steady. Bits of agony shuddered off the page, hard to pick up. When told that Chatty had 'gone from them', despite Catty and Craufurd crying a lot, 'dear May was very still; she did not say much – her quiet mind seemed at once to embrace the gain of death.'

The gain of death.

And the mother Catharine herself a few lines down 'felt indeed that the spirit was gone . . . flown to a region far more suited to it than this world of sin and sorrow.'

Still weak from the birth of Lucy, she suffered the joy of the baptism of the newborn while 'the lifeless form of our beloved child' lay in the very room where Catharine had given birth to them both. And both children at this contorted moment elicited 'thanksgiving'.

Thanksgiving.

The exhausted Catharine wrote, 'I remained in bed all afternoon, trying to realise all that had happened, feeling the greatness of our loss, also the blessedness of having our sweet little one in heaven.'

About what or whom did Tait brood in the plush security of his conveyance? I felt bumped sick by the bus with no mind for anything. The Croydon he bowled through to the clack of hooves was now a shrunk Victorian remnant dominated by today's glassy heights rising out of architect's ego and developer's greed. The old country town, where at times he preached to the privileged, had gone under. His Croydon was archaeology.

The bus drifted through bits of built-up green belt more like environment than country. The flowering cherries had withered on the branch, dropping knickers of lacy pink on to small lawns. The book slithered about on my lap. Catharine was struck by the children's desire to comfort the parents in their loss when Chatty died. By request she recited some verses, which posed an unanswerable question: asked what to offer God to express your love of his gifts, why should it have to be what you most wanted to keep?

The blessedness of having our sweet little one in heaven.

I missed the stop for Addington Palace, which raced past the bus window with a drab hint of minor public school. There was a glimpse of long drive, lined by a skimpy cedar or two, where the Archbishop passed in his carriage. Wan estates ringed the horizons, but Addington remained a small village. The snug church looked endangered only by an office where computer screens glimmered on to the gravestones. Otherwise it was all Trollope on a postcard. A genuine forge was actually in business up the lane. Cottages snoozed under eyebrows of tile. After a steep walk that would have taken it out of the horses, a grand gate flanked by lions loomed.

For a second, breathless, I felt as Tait might, entering his domain, gravel shooting off wheels as the vehicle curved into homecoming. I turned on foot into the driveway. The twin lodges were in place, if closed down. But to the park, to the palace at its zenith, there was no thoroughfare: only a blank wall rank with bushes as overall as weeds. The palace was shut off by brickwork.

The energy ran out of me. The only way into this old palace was from the rear, a mile off, a tradesman's entrance for golfers, choristers, millionaires, whoever ran it now, or admirers of the Taits if they had the puff.

I walked downhill breathing easier into the village with an eye on the pub. With relief I sat at a bench on a patch of grass, accompanied by traffic roaring from a fast road, listening to a place that had given peace to the Taits, now pitilessly stolen by noise that was never going to end. The food tasted half dead, warmed up at speed from the mortuary of a freezer. A thin white wine echoed the sunshine.

The churchyard, which the pub overlooked, was choked with graves edging out of tufts of grass. The tallest object was a fussy obelisk uniting in a last gasp of the Gothic the six archbishops buried close at hand: Benson, whose widow carnally fancied Tait's daughter Lucy; then Manners Sutton, Howley, Sumner, Longley and Tait himself. To accommodate their eminence as well as their names the monument was many-sided, smudged with coats of arms and carvings of mitres. Much of the detail in the soft stone, rising to a point, had been eaten away by weather.

What gap was I trying to bridge? The time gap was not long, the culture gap subtle, the gap of faith between then and now huge – what else? I wanted to communicate with someone who was in theory better than myself in all human respects: to get in touch with a god, indeed God, who was prepared with good grace to descend an airmile or two, to link the empyrean with the quotidian. It was the gap between what lay within me and whatever lay beyond.

I was asking Tait as a man, and Catharine as a woman, and the girls as a family, to indicate to me gifts I was not using, as well as teach me services I could give. On the page they were again taking their last look at Chatty, 'that little form which was that night to be closed from mortal sight'. The wreath on her head, the children's flowers in her two hands, Craufurd's offering on her breast. 'We knelt beside that form in agony,' Catharine said, 'for it was hard to part with her; but strength was given: we felt Whose hand had given, and now had taken her. We know that we shall have her again, though not in this world.' For the most part monosyllables, one at a time to take things in by the sheer force of a need to spell them out. I read it once more and gasped at the punch of it.

At a remove Tait's own tomb stood above a wide oblong of cement below which he lay between wife and son. The memorial looked as nordic as a runestone. At the foot his name was added to theirs as if in after-thought. Beside them was buried yet another daughter with her own unrecorded misery: Agnes Sitwell Tait, m. 2 January, d. 19 December 1888. The dates suggested the span of a pregnancy. Of Lucy, the infant born in 1856 just before the harvest of her sisters, there was no mention on this patch of ground. Her life and death were elsewhere.

A banner announced that the church, otherwise locked, would be open to visitors next Sunday. By luck a couple were arranging flowers. With pride I was shown the Tait window. The three vertical panels of stained glass were more literal than symbolic, St Augustine to the left, Stephen Langton on the right, Archibald Tait in the solemn middle. His pale face looked ashen against strong light from outside, white robes luminous. On a brass plaque the window was dedicated to him 'by the parishioners of Addington as a memorial of their reverence and love'.

Tait bore in this portrait an unsettling resemblance to someone I knew but failed to identify, sternly parental, yet pastoral, if rather sinister. The sun at that instant fading behind a cloud rendered him almost invisible, an invisible man receding into my boyhood, a recollection of fear. He looked pained.

The sloping lawns of Addington Palace were still a golf links. The few cedars were broken or poorly. At a distance the house retained a bleak grandeur, a whale of the past beached on a fragmented present. Afternoon accidie, assisted by that white wine, dried my tongue.

Meanwhile I could just imagine Tait's relief on trotting in a doze of numinous reflection past the lion gates home – there to embrace Catharine, an irresistible object in an immovable world.

At the bus stop groups of schoolchildren hung about. The top of my bus was crammed with youth high in mood and pitch, pumping vitality into the badinage of growing up. A bald chap in his forties did his best to snooze; I felt deafened and uplifted. I kept tight hold of my book, where another child's death was expected at any minute. At East Croydon my bus pass was valid for Victoria: the thrill of an hour's journey by road reduced by rail to ten minutes: progress.

On the train I found that after the first girl's death in the Carlisle Deanery the infant Susan insisted at Sunday school on occupying the chair left free for her missing sister – all too much for Catharine, close to breakdown, trying to keep fear at bay: 'Just then there rushed to my heart a feeling of separation from them which I could not bear, and an intense faintness.' And there came upon her the notion – 'unable to fix my thoughts' – that she herself would be the next to go.

As the train rattled towards Victoria, braking through thickets of suburb towards Clapham Junction, rows of bedroom windows winking in the late sunlight touched off a reminder: the shared wealth of dreams all over London which had a common purpose beyond our grasp. I thought too of another likelihood: love being nurtured more in the dreaming mind than either consciously or as an illusory result of the sex drive. And without thinking, or thinking only of Catharine, it struck me: the idea that the mass of dreams could produce an archive of human experiences to match the size of the universe or fill in its holes, an archive which might take up no space at all. And then I dozed awake as we ground into the shadow of the terminus.

Five

And there was that sexual event in my boyhood. It took place ninety minutes from London by rail. I had to consult it before further clearing the air to be in more touch with the Taits than research was letting me. It stuck unrealised in my mind, that rearing of sex: the moment when a childlike possibility of faith in me (or so memory made it seem) was thwarted by the ugly need of an adult who started as a hero, became a god, looked a creep and turned out a devil.

I walked the twelve minutes from home to Waterloo. The next train to Alton, where as a boy I spent most of the war, started half full and emptied out bit by bit towards its terminus at the market town in Hampshire that was my birthplace. I alighted alone, along with ghosts of others.

The eye of memory saw the place as not just shrunk, but diminished. A nucleus survived: the church, the terrace of shapely mansions down Crown Hill, scraps of the High Street. But gaps gaped. Out of them drifted waves of amnesia. I hovered between an inability and a reluctance to recollect just what stood where in the war years. The landmarks I knew directed me from one site of devastation to the next. Shopfronts had been torn down for the glassy swathe of a supermarket. A district of lanes packed with working-class cottages narrowing to the rear of Normandy Street had been razed to admit the speed of an inner ring road. Grey estates crawled over the remembered blue of my boyhood hills.

But I was in search of something more positive than the spoliation of a place. I wanted my brush with faith back.

In the parish church I had sung in the choir from the London blitz in 1940 until VE Day in 1945, as treble, alto, bass. At first glance little had changed. The grave-yard had been landscaped; choirboys could no longer play hide-and-seek among the tombstones, which had been removed. A few had been ranked in gloomy parade against the wall of Miss Tew's grand Victorian house. The grass looked badly shaved under skimpy pines sadly in need of replacement. I stared up at the slatted windows of the belfry below the steeple. At least those narrow but emotive orifices were still in place. In the porch the door with the Roundhead bullet hole from the Civil War swung into the nave with a loud report. The past was open.

Once inside there seemed no way upwards. Surely the spiral stairs to the tower started somewhere in the half-dark under the wealth of Norman arches that held it up. The frontage of the organ looked much the same, though surely the display pipes used to have scrolls of text gilded across their magnificence. But the position of the console, where we practised behind the baize curtain on winter nights, was a blank, unlike my clean memory of it. Plainly rebuilding, financed by an appeal, had moved the console somewhere out into the body of the church.

I stood where the keyboards had once been, and my early history again unrolled. The assistant choirmaster swung his legs off the stool. With a flutter of his fingers, mistakable for a blessing by anyone not in the know, he dismissed the choir. He gave me a slack nod, as of approval, and raised a palm to hold me back. The others skittered off through the vestry to shout in the last of the sun outside among the gravestones.

Without a word the man entered the cavernous space where the bell ropes hung beneath the tower. His manner was remote, the chancel twilit. He appeared hardly more present than a ghost, a man becoming invisible by the second.

With a whack he unlocked a door. A spiral iron stair lifted from the shadows towards a blur of acid light. The man stood aside. It appeared I was to mount the steps ahead of him. My knees pistoned up the rungs. Below me he whistled a snatch of anthem between his teeth with excess of spit in it. I arrived among the bells in huge awe of their magnitude. The sub-organist slapped one in passing. It emitted a flat clang.

What was all this for? There was no delay, no time to think. The man, neck weakly cricked back, swerved towards me, eyes faint under the glasses, gazing up into woodwormed beams, and slid his hands over the flannels of my backside and began rotating his pelvis round my tummy as if by massage to remove a pain. I sniffed old sweat seeping out of utility cloth. My stomach pinched up, about to retch or contort with giggles.

The rub against my abdomen swelled. What should I do now? I looked askance at the slats of the window cut into the stone wall. A dust of sunlight lay on the ancient cement close to my eye. This was my one narrow escape into the outside world.

Without comment the man withdrew a pace and

fumbled with the buttons of the school trousers I was wearing. They dropped to my ankles. So did my pants, gusset soiled. I edged nearer to the safe slant of the window. Pained intakes of breath snorted above my head. Knees moved in a furry caress against my upper thighs. It was all new and smelt adult. The rough shirt and loosely knotted tie pressed into my face. I pulled slightly back for fear of being smothered. A bristly chin pricked my temple.

The man's hard thing was pulled up naked against my tummy button. Its skin slithered with insistence against skin. For me it was all beyond likelihood. Not happening. Eyes blindly averted, the man half bent, ready, knees at a low angle, steady, as for the start of a race, go, and he manhandled his swollen member into the space between my legs.

To and fro he began to pump it, trying to prime an engine, in a temper for not getting it to start. His rage fumed on, his head swaying back and forth, his open mouth silently telling off the world. Fury gargled in his nose.

I tried gradually to pull away. I found I could glimpse downwards at a clumsy angle the spread of Miss Tew's garden far below, a jumble of rooftops, ranks of chimneys uppermost, a wide strip of lawn, all foreshortened, as sickening as an abyss, but also as safe as houses.

I felt I was falling. The throat pressed to my temple hawked up breath at the same tempo as the thrust between my legs. It beat at my head, coughing up pain. I got a vertiginous glimpse of daffodils. A clump of lilac swayed in the breeze. The flat fingers of the sub-organist were on my hips. The hands were my prison.

Only my head was free, the corner of my eye. At my ear the breath came short. A sunset glared into one of the slats, at which point he quickly stood back, eyes more glazed than ever, breath coarse, and spurted into the air above a pistoning hand a pearly stream of wet.

'That's what you put into a woman to get a baby,' he asserted jerkily.

Never had he been more outspoken or sounded more like gospel truth. The gospel had just shuddered on to the floorboards. It mingled with the dust and made common cause with the woodworm. The smell of the gospel was acrid. It looked like opaque jelly, this testament, a pallid blancmange. A bit of holy writ dripped on to my underpants as I pulled them up. A postscript to the divine message flicked on to my trousers as I buttoned my flies.

The assistant choirmaster looked anywhere but at me as he adjusted his dress. He ground his heel on enough seed to populate half the county. I tried for a last glance at the vertical drop from the tower, but the gardens had skulked into night. The sub-organist was already halfway down the ladder, his baldness descending. I felt my way after him down the ladder, then dizzily round the spiral stairway, until I reached the unsteady plane of now unreadable memorials beneath my feet. Somehow the act had contradicted the gathering blackness of the church. The act was too interesting to me to notice at once that it freed me: I no longer needed to believe in any such things as the dumb language of music or the organ's quiet innards. I was shot of the numinous.

Six

More than half a century later I came out of the church into elderly daylight. The mansion I had looked down on from the tower had long vanished beneath housing. The vicarage opposite, for two ample centuries a retreat in warm brick complete with stableyard, had also gone. A villa for the vicar took up a tenth of its space. Vicarage Hill had been widened yards to turn a lane into a highway. On every side the human dimension felt diminished. I stood looking at spaces which on one level or another I had once as a boy solidly occupied. They were now thin air.

Here in this church I had reported sermons for the local paper at a thousand words a week. I sat in my stall taking covert notes on paper hidden in the folds of my surplice. I had to catch the drift of the vicar's thoughts, pin down vagaries of logic. I envied that wizened figure composing them in the study long demolished over-looking pensive lawns now built over, at his right hand a decanter of sherry even drier than his voice. From the pulpit the sermons sounded as wise as faith. It never occurred to me that they might be recycled from an earlier parish, even from abandoned beliefs, or revived from a dead age.

Writing them down felt like believing in them. They must come from heaven above.

'The reality and nearness of the world unseen.'

In that echo of Tait's boyhood, I now saw my young self in a cassock taking notes from on high. First I jotted down revelations, then hurried home to expand them in manuscript, for the benefit of those who had absented themselves from the felicity of matins. With my help the local rag was spreading the word. My secular friend who edited the paper never cut a comma for fear of giving offence to all concerned, in particular the vicar.

Yet every matins the vicar preached to a congregation of the deaf. The portly newsagent was more interested in his lunch than in the food for thought delaying it. In the front pews the teenage girls I fancied, nylon knees clamped above their hassocks, stared ahead at an altar that had more promise of marriage than prospect of faith in it. Condemned during the sermon to a spell without music, the sub-organist floated with half-closed eyes on a doze of desire for the ranks of boys. The ritual was timelessly repeated weekly. The vicar droned while I scribbled while nobody listened while minutes vanished. The words ran in and out of faith as blindly as mice.

For I too missed what the vicar was talking about, even if I was reporting it. Somewhere, lost in places I had long since left, were the cuttings pasted by my parents into a scrapbook. I would never locate them; nor would I ever consult the *Hampshire Herald*'s files in Winchester. Those distant reports from across the divide had sent my beliefs packing into the void of manhood.

Only in the last week had I discovered how sermons came to hand and to mind. Into Randall Davidson's two-volume biography of Tait was folded a page of foolscap in facsimile. It illustrated Tait's way of preparing an address. He quartered the paper into narrow columns, numbering the sequences into which his speech would fall. With a scratchy pen he put down his headings, enough to strike off apt phrasing. He knew too that a good speaker took one look at the audience to know exactly how to slant his remarks. Notes were insurance against adrenalin failing to hit. A hundred scribbled words or less were expected to fill half an hour or more with whatever it was: a message from the invisible, a welcome to overseas bishops, an appeal for money. With that folded paper in his hand, probably unconsulted, Tait never doubted his word or the Word.

It struck me as unlikely to be here in Alton, repository of a faithful boyhood, that I regained an understanding of faith or heard the call. For I knew that sooner or later, in the choir club where on Friday nights we made balsa wood models of warships or in the midst of a piano lesson on Monday afternoons or by some coincidence during the week that suited him, the sub-organist would again lead me away with a nod into a place to which he had the key. The invisible man: the something or someone I still saw over my shoulder after all these years.

The sub-organist hung about that Hampshire town. He appeared to be of no fixed address, but had the keys to almost anywhere. My sexual image of him is bending sideways to fit unfamiliar keys into locks that clicked with threat. He amazed me as a mixture of the unknowable, the unsavoury, and the unseen. For weeks, when the choirmaster himself (who was often ill) officiated at practice, his deputy sloped off into spheres of his own. Others claimed to have glimpsed him cycling broodily down a back street, but very seldom. I once saw him, or someone like him, amble into a bank, but though I waited half an hour, idling on my own bike, he never reappeared; I later found that the bank had an exit through the manager's garden past a watercress bed.

Certainly it was never clear what the sub-organist did for a living. Grown-ups spoke of him as if he were a pillar of society, but soon stopped talking about him, as if his name were dangerous. I began to think irrationally that he would only appear in my life at an angle, at the wrong time of day, when he had sudden wants. And surely I was not alone, he must equally appear at odd intervals to others, choirboys, schoolboys, paperboys, the town's prepubertal riff-raff who, half on bikes, half off, whizzed about the market square in quest of adventure or purpose. The sub-organist was a secret we were never supposed to mention, my yet unissued passport to maturity.

And now today a last look at my old haunts. Where the vicarage hayloft had stood, where I personally had stood on its rickety boards being interfered with, was a piece of limitless sky. I stared into something that had become nothing. The outside gents to the rear of the Crown Hotel, where he eased my bottom against cold tiles, had been converted into an extension of the themed bar. A dental surgery, into which he had whipped me wordlessly one urgent afternoon, was now some commuter's kitchen. The geography of his libido was no longer on the map.

One institution unsullied by memory of the sub-organist, the Swan Hotel, struck me as the best spot in town to wipe him out with a drink. I leant at the bar staring into a glass of red wine that caught a shifting sunbeam, tinged by a bottle-green window above the door: an effect of stained glass suggesting a memorial. In church a particular girl's nylon knees clamped in prayer had later been pulled apart as she swung in tight breeches on to a horse. Even now in age I felt a tingle of desire.

When I emptied the glass the last of the colour drained out. I ordered a refill which less fully caught the light. My mind fell short of the girl's name. But I remembered the rising interest in my loins as a novelty of unforeseeable peril. I felt it as exciting in implication as the war quietly tick-tocking in this backwater of a town. The image of her kneeling in church, hands veiling her face, her long red coat a cassock, made me so aware that I was missing some richer ingredient in this ascetic feast of memories that I ordered yet another glass of burgundy. I could doze my head off in the train home. The archive needed a bit of hypnogogic input.

And then on the twilit way up to the station, a little groggy, with a last look over my shoulder at the distant church, there strayed into my mind a fact unbelievably forgotten. The sub-organist was a man of few words. But one night in mid-war, staying me with a finger after choir practice, he muttered that he had got something here for me I might like. The remark had his usual nod of threat. Too close for comfort we were standing in the vestry. I could hear my fellows shouting off into the freedom of the dusk, but here the cassocks stacked behind sliding doors smelt of the senility of basses who smoked pipes. The threat loomed as he began fumbling among sheets of surplices, trousers flapping, and I waited in a dumb paralysis of obedience to be beckoned and debagged.

Abruptly he turned and passed me a book.

He looked elsewhere, told me to hurry off, rolled his eyes in despair, hustled me out, put the big key in the lock, and flapped a hand at me yards off as he hastened towards his bike. And all I could do was stare, in disbelieving gratitude, at this book called *The Organ Viewed from Within*. I had been casually handed a bible by a pontiff.

In minutes, straining my eyes under the graveyard trees, I grasped the extent of his generosity. This was a primer, a handbook to the mechanism of the organ, with fifty-two illustrations and diagrams (one for every week in the year), by John Broadhouse, an instant hero and savant, author of *How to Make a Violin*, whose fifteen chapters (one daily for over a fortnight) had such breathtaking titles as 'Wind Supply', 'From Key to Pallet' and 'How the Grooves are Arranged', all published by William Reeves, no less immediate a hero, at 83 Charing Cross Road, London, W.C.2. And beginning at the first words, 'Most people have seen an organist on his seat', I walked reading the gospel through the back streets of our town, down the alleys where the gangs skulked, into the scare of an air raid warning, past noise from the pubs, across a meadow no doubt about to be bombed, and so home, where I laid it on the altar of my pillow and within sound of the all clear turned to the peroration on the last page. 'It has been well and truly said that there is no finality in organ building,' said Broadhouse with biblical simplicity. 'It is difficult to see what further even electricity can do for the organ; but when we compare the first locomotive with a Great Northern express engine, a Montgolfier balloon with an aeroplane, or a "growler" with a powerful Daimler, it would be rash to say that nothing further can be done. In this department, as in so many others, we must "wait and see".'

I decided there and then, for as long as I could or had to, not only to wait and see, but to fall back on the past because I liked it and to make up the future as I went along. With a book such as *The Organ Viewed from Within* between my fingers the present could look after itself.

To offer thanks for this munificence was out of order. Never again did the sub-organist mention the book. Nor did I.

Part III

One

A day or two later we drove to Oxford to visit our daughter, who was attending a sixth-form college, and we stayed overnight with an old friend in Walton Street. As usual in a bed away from home, I dreamed in a strange tense, as if some linguist in a next-door bedroom were altering the grammar of my shut-eye. Down the dark street, turn left, then right, loomed the caricature Gothic of Balliol, of which in Tait's spell as a tutor I was half thinking when I nodded off, his biography at my side.

I dreamed of nothing so factual as that among Tait's pupils were numbered Victorian giants like Matthew Arnold, whose father's job as headmaster Tait was to take over at Rugby. That fact I gleaned from the book; facts never stood the test of dreams. I then shaved in a mirror that showed me nothing beyond my tattered self, except a reflection of Oxford on a spring morning that looked more remembered than true. At breakfast I was already looking forward to strolling the immemorial streets, as though I owned them. Even the spires were dreaming for once.

Thus it was my daughter who prompted this fresh opportunity to stare into Tait's privacy. Here I was, in his Oxford, in his youth. Meanwhile, in memory's eye, and from snapshots at home, I saw her at all the stages at which Catharine's daughters had died. I thought back to our daughter as an infant of genius, a toddler prodigy, a grown-up four-year-old, an eager teenager of seven or eight, a little girl of ten almost too old to be an adult: the whole pack. At these ages, subtly altering appearance as the months passed, she grew up on and off in the Wales we were now selling, a country still as still as the nineteenth century.

The young Tait's road started from the gate of Balliol on a Saturday much like this. Marsh Baldon, the outlying parish he took on when a classics don in 1836, seemed miles as well as years away. Across Folly Bridge, I traced him through an endless series of round-abouts linked by roads snaking into developments that looked unlived in. At length these half-suburbs turned into scraps of countryside just surviving the urban greed for greenery. In his time the journey was a trudge into the lyrical: five miles on foot on Saturday, trotting to and fro on horseback in mid-week. He was under no pressure, save from a keen conscience, to go to all this trouble to serve the souls of a gnarled handful of yokels. He believed in their right to salvation. He believed in them. But why?

O God by whom the meek are guided in judgment, Tait's boyhood had been stuffed with indoctrination in Thy name. His psyche grew up knowing it needed daily doses of the drug which only faith in Thee could inject. From faith sprang his application: a phenomenal power to study with diligence, to do well in the world without succumbing to worldliness. He trod so carefully up the ladder that pride was always one step ahead of hubris.

I was driving out into unknown country. Swathes of Oxfordshire I had never travelled when up at Christ Church encircled the car. My own ambition in those days was jerked alive as much by blind ego as by the false god of self-expression. To work at all, as well as to function as a man in the round, Tait had early required an aim beyond himself. He believed all his efforts were made for a higher purpose, an uncheckably divine one. Otherwise the inherent selfishness of all effort, and all achievement, showed up too much. There was already an element in Tait of the communicator. He wanted to have his say; but he insisted it be or feel inspired.

At the wheel my mind wobbled between recollections. One foot close to the clutch, the other accelerating, I thought of Archie Tait born with his feet doubled inwards; without help he would never have walked. Moving at 60mph on to a ring road, I found memory hovering over a journey from Edinburgh in search of a cure when Archie was seven. By sea from Leith to Hull, with day after day hardly a breath of wind, took more than a week, food running out, whereupon they had to tack up the Trent to Gainsborough, there disembarking to post westwards to Renishaw Hall, the Sitwell pile where in 1818 Archie's elder sister Susan had married Sir George. What in my life came within a jaw-cracking yawn of matching such aggressive tedium as that pain of a journey?

But, down to a crawl at roadworks, I slowed into a recent example. Only three boats a week at awkward hours of day or night plied to and from the isle of Colonsay off the west coast of Scotland. Rising from warm beds in cold weather before 5 a.m. to drive north from Carlisle, drawing comfort of mind only from a heated car, taking an aeon to reach and circumvent Glasgow, curving round the rocky edges of lochs in the half-light, wipers washing, watching out of the corner of a tired eye hotels slowly opening to drab breakfasts overlooking sheets of water, staring up at shivers of snow unmelted on the heights, driving on year after year with scarcely a sign of traffic for mile upon mile, the car eating up only a fraction of the bulk of Scotland, the children fretful from starvation in the back, and descending towards a scribble of inlets where small vessels were tugging at anchor, the rain clearing by now as houses at odd angles loomed out of the diminishing mist, and we steered down as if making landfall into Oban: a wet snake of a high street before shops opened, a quay with grey naval patrols tied up, then on foot at last into the booking hall where for a good sum you at last guaranteed your car, your family, yourself, a passage to Colonsay leagues over the sea.

I waited for tickets in the queue. Somewhere in that backward wilderness behind us lay old Mrs Rutherford's house, where Archie spent his crucial night in 'the reality and nearness of the world unseen'.

By now it was 9.30 a.m. and we had been up for the neural equivalent of a fortnight; the relief of bumping over gangplanks on to the ship, the pleasure of finding hot tea, the ease of watching sea at speed swill past the spotted glass of the view towards and between islands untold and unnamed. The apparent month or so it took to Colonsay, long enough to achieve an inner rumble of the timeless, ended with a pint of beer, as this island, definition of ultimate solitude, shuddered closer. The engines roared down and died. We drove out on to a small pier where our host had been loitering for an age in the hope of a delivery of oysters. The voyage had taken all of three hours.

The island was rock. The heights were bleak. On the

Atlantic side the beaches cut into the coast – tunnels of wind that forced blurred tears. Yet swathes of sand blazed yellow, the blue of an early weed or red of a wildflower cropping up warmed the eye against the cold. On the tops I felt buffeted by wave on wave of emotion at its stormiest. I was being blown about a place where I might have come for solace if I had lost children or where children might die. On every walk a wind with 3000 miles of ocean behind it came howling round an unexpected corner to almost knock me off my feet. These extremes, highest wind and most cutting cold, sent me quickly back to the house drained, to fall at once on my host's comforts of affection and wine.

In temperature this Easter at Colonsay House lasted the full span of a Victorian winter. Our bodies were unused to the bite of cold; those of the Taits a century ago were inured. With increasing pleasure, as I explored the shapes and sizes of its apartments, I equated this fusty accumulation of a residence with what I imagined of Tait's Deanery in Carlisle, a house where fireplaces could be stoked with never quite enough logs to puff more heat than smoke at the pious toes pointed towards them in slippers. In the surrounds of that remotest of English cathedrals the silence can have been no less absolute. It had messages to convey far beyond the noise of the rest of life. I lay in bed and heard it, we walked out into the forest of rhododendrons and heard it, it penetrated the head: despite the lure of this silence it contained a language none of us seemed yet to have learnt.

For more than a week on Colonsay we were cut off from all but domestic communication. Gossip drizzled round the island as foggily as the weather. Good people

– a casual girl in the pub, a farmer with a past – were magnified into figures of legend, whores or devils. Scale changed: individuals loomed in the island smallness, yet looked tiny against wind and weather. Given the absence of servants at the house, living on Colonsay today was the spit of life on the mainland a century or more ago: that intense degree of being settled for good in one place, the uncertainty of communications if not their total lack, being involuntarily at the mercy of the elements. In grave reflection I huddled and scuttled about the place living a senior clergyman's life in a huge past that had tipped generously into the present. I felt released into a copy of Tait's world.

In the same frame of timeless stasis, a few days later, after taking the fragile link to the mainland, the ferry running ages late, and driving into the small hours through a Glasgow reflected off the lamplit damp of its bare thoroughfares, we arrived in bed close to Carlisle far too late for the next day to seem real or for any future to look likely. Even my resolve to visit, if possible, the 'dingy old Deanery', as Tait called it, was thwarted by my need to come back with a bang into my own century and go home whimpering to London comfort. The present Dean wasn't at home. There wasn't time. Again the past had slipped me by.

Down to Tait's village curacy in the Baldons the lane, shaggily marked as wooded on the old map, still had lots of trees. Beyond and above them swung the march of the hyper pylons; their feet curling into the earth, their heads pronging the heavens, the slings of cable carrying today's light into dark places. But in the hamlet of Toot Baldon, where the littler of Tait's churches lay hidden at a remove, a couple of people on horseback clopping in and out of shadow preceded me down the avenue, slowly riding the entire place into anachronism.

The weather intercut slaps of wind with flushes of sunlight, as Tait's road into Marsh Baldon debouched on to a cricket ground side-whiskered by tall grasses. For a village green it was immense. Far away round its borders opened a fan of houses that muddled styles and periods, thatch nudging slate, red-brick next door to pebbledash, stringing together centuries of architectural fad and folly: an England. Nobody was about. Horses grazed at a distance. The several cars parked at intervals were camouflaged by shrubbery. Little more than a chrome bumper offered a gleam of our own century.

I stopped, switched off, breathed the rough air. 'I cannot but remember how, when a curate in a small village in Oxfordshire,' Tait said, 'I marvelled at the excitement raised in a quiet and dull place by a gathering of the Methodists on a fine summer's day on the Common, under the shadow of the old trees; how the voice of their preacher, sounding through the stillness of a listening crowd, and the burst of their hymns pealing far and wide through the village, seemed well suited to attract and raise the hearts of many who never entered within the Church to join in its measured devotion, and listen to its calm teaching.'

Tait's main church here in Marsh Baldon shared canopies of trees with a manor house in an even more sempiternally English class of setting. A pretty pair of girls shepherded by parents emerged from the church-yard with dogs on leads. A pets service in honour of St Francis had just taken place. Within the nave plump spinsters were drinking coffee under a sombre oil of the Annunciation. On a return visit in 1872 the then Archbishop Tait wrote in his diary, 'I found the old church of Marsh Baldon in the same state as when I preached my first sermon in it in 1836. All the old people whom I knew are dead, and I could recognise but few of the younger . . .' The vicar moved towards me with an air of welcome. The coffee smelled as alien as incense. I fled into the rain until things quietened down, turning on the wipers.

In the car I gathered up what I recollected of Tait's youth. It felt as though I were remembering it as personal experience: myself when young. I could hear the thud of obituary in its measured ambition. That silent night in a strange lodging in Scotland; thereafter, in his passage through the Edinburgh Academy to become head boy, whether snatching the choice prizes at Glasgow University or winning an exhibition to Balliol, few signs of any but the dourest humour glowed. Archie swotted. Neither time ill spent below nor further revelation from on high figured in his young life. He worked fourteen hours a day. No doubt he had to work longer hours than cleverer men to force the best from himself. My mood in the car felt shadowed by the awesomely boring ordinariness of virtue.

Yet Tait's aspirations kept calling and calling on God. He needed guidance lest his longing to rise in the world overpower his desire to save it. Even his successes in study hinted at a mediocrity that was endearing. He was a scholar but no visionary; a force for good without imagination. At Oxford I would have found him as much a prig as myself.

From the evidence of men he taught, I recalled that Tait had difficulty in unstiffening or taking things lightly. Pupils and peers awarded him the good old adjectives of 'robust' and 'manly', intended as high compliments but sounding nowadays like reservations. Yet there was a purity, sheer niceness almost, in his self-searching (which he imposed only on his diary) that lent him charm not far short of charisma. He was certainly shy; I knew from adolescence and beyond how the grip of that minor paralysis hurt. His sermons were described as 'sincere' or 'worthy', two more well-meant adjectives that sounded the knell. His Oxford lectures on moral philosophy, not to mention classical texts, stretched the attention span even of his own century to snapping point. And then suddenly at thirty-two he succeeded Dr Arnold as headmaster of Rugby.

What did he look like? In Davidson's life the frontispiece image of Tait at Rugby, in those early Victorian years of sketchy portraiture, offered a young man with sloping shoulders in the academic gear of the time, curly lightish hair not untidy but in moderate disorder, brow not too high but a long face in which each feature – wan eyes, strong nose, sensual mouth – added up to a whole of reserve, perception, kindness; and, far behind, puzzlement – most of what a man might need these days, virtues seductive enough to lure forth faith. He also looked sexy.

Rain still fell. Embracing this parish might have relieved Tait from the worst of his public fight against the Oxford Movement. For he took on, head-on, John Henry Newman and his Tracts for the Times. With no vicarage he slept Saturday nights in a rented cottage, but had to hasten back to Balliol in time for the Sunday afternoon service in college. In advance he was always berating himself for his failure to live up to responsibilities – whether to his twenty students, or later to the 500 boys at Rugby, or afterwards, when a bishopric came his way, to the entire population of London. He kept regretting being too busy to make time for private prayer. Prayer was the mind's holiday from the mundane. Prayer was an escape from the world with a view to improving it.

But impulses more than half worldly ate into Tait's character. He was satisfied with the status quo, yet his mind was hungry for reform. His trips abroad in the long Oxford vacations, onerous journeys up and down Europe in a tumble of coaches, to Germany and Italy, were assault courses on culture. He felt impelled to find out in record time how education, politics, religion, worked in alien climes. He was merciless in self-improvement. Despite any amount of doubt he was sure he was right. This made action easy to initiate as well as quick to achieve. The sweetness of his outward rectitude was cut by the acidity of his inner anxiety: he was the very model of a good man in a bad way.

The vicar's car muttered off into silence. Not a soul was to be seen anywhere near the church. In the porch a sundial was attached to the stonework over the south door. A medieval reminder of time so long gone as to be hardly traceable, it now stood vertical and in permanent shadow, beyond the reach of both time and light. The scratchy code of numerals ringing its circumference was scarcely visible. I had to strain upwards to see it in any detail and at that moment my neck cricked, a sharp little nag of pain crossing the base of the skull, the sundial stirring in me an unplumbable depth of feeling: a trance less like the present moment than a future dream.

I stood for a long spell, as if struck dumb by a knowledge that might slip my grasp. Yes, if this were not yet a dream, I felt it must be raw material for one. I was spying on it, the key ingredient in an episode of that activity that took place in the brain at dead of night: dreaming. And I knew it. In today's daylight I was glimpsing the point of an event that might happen only in darkness behind closed eyes.

Stumbling back into time, I entered the little church. Up tiny steps, from the eminence of the Jacobean pulpit, in which young Tait preached, I pictured more or less what he must have seen: not many people with not much faith, suffering their time without complaint. From this modest eminence he was offering them the wider community he himself enjoyed, the deeper spirit he believed in, the privilege of God's cruelty. I had none of these advantages or rights. With a shiver I stepped down from the pulpit into an unprincipled void.

But there was an organ. It was oddly placed at the rear of the church. The four-square instrument (built by J. W. Walker, late 1880s) had not existed in Tait's time. Lifting the unlocked lid revealed two manuals. The yellowing of the ivory stops with the scuffed print of their names in black brought into play, with force, my boyhood of hunting out hidden organs in Hampshire during the war. I stared and stared at it, almost tearful, sure that something was about to occur, a click, a clue. Then slowly I saw that the answer was hidden somewhere behind the conflict between the organ's music and that man, damn the man, who revealed its might to me, who shifted in and out of the alleys of our town on who knew what shady enterprises, retreating into nowhere at the slightest sign of threat.

Marsh Baldon during Tait's curacy was a backwater of rustic torpor; he wasted his faith on it. I preferred the place now, neat and faithless, its spirit nodding off in the armchair of the present. But neither of these versions of death could I really bear, since I had the capacity to enliven neither. I trudged back down an avenue of chestnuts towards the car which offered no escape. I still felt the sub-organist looming out of space and time, busying himself with some triviality that would lead to the summons as he slipped sidelong into the vestry.

That evening back in Oxford, a city where naturally man thought more of immortality than of death, we dined with friends overlooking a garden lapping down to the river. One dear woman I had known for over half a century; we shared an early romance. Now she had lost her only son in a motorbike accident. At table her air of absence touched off Catharine's presence, making as little social effort as was seemly, picking at food and talk. Here was Mrs Tait sitting in polite agony. Her familiar face lay spent in sorrow, as round the table we all jingled the small change of culture in the dusk.

At Oxford nothing accustomed us as students to loss or death. The obituary of a statesman in the news-papers not only made him somewhat ridiculous but made room for someone younger. Our infantile view of death sprang from cinema: a cult composed of corpses leaping into the air riddled with bullets or droves of the middle-class middle-aged sinking in torpedoed liners. Death was a laugh. A don vanishing, and we breathed more freely: at least someone had been prevented for good from teaching us how to think or behave. Here and now, over the last of the wine, I looked out into the late wan green of the evening and thought how limited I had always been, or wrong, most of the time, about nearly everything.

In youth I rarely came across even a hint of death. A mouth you were kissing had little death in it, unless you hit unlucky: halitosis, cheap perfume at the worst. Skin textures, lit by those Oxford suns that would never sink except into all-night sessions, looked as if time had no power to dim their sheen. The Oxford buses safely ran over only old people. Parties in jam-packed rooms were as alive as a world constructed from scratch. The erotic arose on carpets in front of gas fires in rooms in college with the oak sported and privacy guaranteed: in particular the low-lit thighs that always obsessed Walter, the curves of a bottom, the novelty of coition with most of our clothes on; on numerous occasions Walter never bothered even to lower his trousers. We had history on our side without knowing it.

The university was the universe, with not a microcosm in sight. Yet just round the corner at Balliol, given a little imagination, I might have found Archie Tait in the same stupor as mine before any woman was served or baby born, sharing my utter innocence. In young Oxford death was a distinction gained only when your ambition had earned the right to it.

I now stared at the rusty stonework of Balliol where Tait tutored. The very windows framed a narrowly intellectual slant on the world. Tait had a good Oxford, and Balliol men always regarded their careers, if not with the 'effortless superiority' of Benjamin Jowett's phrase, then with an assumption of relentless progress; 'One man is as good as another,' as the same Balliol master put it, 'until he has written a book.' Tait had taught Jowett as well as such shakers of the Victorian future as Arthur Hugh Clough. And they all wrote books.

In the Broad opposite Tait's college stood the narrow, tall, toppling chaos of Thornton's, where as students we used to rummage for book bargains. In the rear stacks, winding my way through to Theology, I looked for Catharine's testimony at rest in the muddle of a library sold or an attic junked. Sure enough, within a hundred yards of Tait's college, in good condition and priced at £28, his wife's anguish bound in faded olive-green cloth was for sale. With shock I thought of all their life being only on paper. For good or ill they had quit the known world for good. A few hieroglyphs within the asylum of hard covers were all that was left. And I also thought I ought to be able to think better than this, and to more point.

So I concentrated on the idea of young Tait across the road; I tried to remember myself when young in this street, and slipped briefly into a specious warp, looking forward to Tait's future. A few years on, Archibald Campbell Tait would be married to Catharine Spooner. Within five years (1842) he was to be headmaster of Rugby following Arnold. 'I quite quake for the awful responsibility,' wrote a friend and mentor, 'putting on that giant's armour. However, I really believe you are far the best. My main fears are for your sermons being dull, and your Latin prose, and composition generally, weak, in which latter points you will have, I think, hard work. But I earnestly say, as far as we can see, "God grant he may get it!".' And get it Tait did; judging by the syntax and sentiments of the above, without much help from his friends.

Within a further seven years (1849) he was to be Dean of Carlisle. 'Your reputation for learning and sound divinity', wrote Lord John Russell in October, 'have induced me to propose to you to recommend you to the Queen for the vacant Deanery of Carlisle . . .' And get that he did too, despite the even more tortured dubiety hidden in the official grammar.

I squatted in a corner of Theology, student legs passing my eyeline at intervals. Weighing Catharine in my hand, wondering whether to buy her, I opened my find at random. I crouched on piles of unwanted books, and I read. I read of the death of their children. I shrank to let others much younger squeeze past into more modern departments, and I read more. And here in 1990s Oxford I was still thinking of Archie as present and correct in 1840s Oxford. She had not yet met Archie, yet they were already in grief. The children were not yet conceived, but now they were dead. In a scarcely articulate depth of my own mind every word I was reading was a prayer, or a mixture of prayer and oracle, or a confusion of oracle and prayer and death wish. For a second I seemed in danger of under-standing time.

So years on from here and now in Oxford their daughter Susan, who was hardly two, was dying, five days after her sister Chatty, in 1856, 'on Tuesday, March 11th,' said Catharine on my knee, 'and in sadness and bitterness of heart we went together to the drawing-room and sat there. I never saw my little lamb again. A few hours after, when her Father saw her laid on her little bed, calm and peaceful, the face had regained some of the beauty it had lost in the conflict with death. I never have been able to realise how the other darlings bore the tidings. We were now entirely separated from them, as at seven o'clock in the morning they had been taken to another house. How greatly did this necessary separation increase to us the agony! I longed for communion with those darlings, I longed to strengthen and cheer them, and anxious, most anxious, I felt as to what my Catty might suffer, as I knew she would realise all that was going on, and would long to come to me and her Father for help and comfort. But we left her and all of them in God's hand, who had thus come among us, and was taking to Himself our beautiful ones, whom we had had such delight in training for Him.

'On Wednesday the 12th, soon after three o'clock, our little Susan was laid in the same grave which had received her Chatty on the Monday. From one window in my room I saw her carried out, and from the other I saw my darlings at Mr Gipp's house opposite, looking at me with faces I can never forget. After a few minutes of watching each other we both withdrew to read again that solemn Service . . .

'Darling Francie had been anxious for some little time that I should teach her to read and to work,' Catharine went on, 'and I pictured to myself the comfort I should find in this occupation. But this was not to be. Friday, I watched them from the Deanery windows as they walked together in the Abbey, and in the afternoon went to look at them through the window of Mr Gipp's house. All sprang to the window and held up the pictures they were painting for us to see. Little Frances was very anxious that we should admire her donkey, but Mamma's eyes were fixed on *her*, and sweet she looked, and very well. We wished them all good-night, and early in the morning received good accounts of them all. It was Saturday, March 15th. After our sad trouble I felt most anxious again to go to church. I had been absent four Sundays; so we talked together about this, and wondered if it would be right – if we might venture – and determined to refer the matter to Mr Page, who would soon come in.

'On Wednesday, just before the funeral of our little Susan, we had removed dear Cousin Nannie to a nice quiet lodging near, in which she could be kept out of the fearful currents of air which we now kept in the Deanery to prevent infection; also it seemed desirable to disperse as much as possible, as, though we hoped the best, no one could tell what might be before us.

'About eleven o'clock that Saturday morning the Dean came back to the drawing-room and Mr Page with him. I was just beginning to ask about our going to church, when he said, "No, dear, that is taken out of our hands, for we fear Frances is ill." She had been sitting on Catty's knee after breakfast, hearing a story, when she was taken with sudden sickness.'

I snapped shut the pages and staggered to my feet. Putting out a hand, I dislodged a tumble of books, and had to have help while the cramp eased from a young woman buying a Penguin classic, and then I queued and paid. I now had my own Catharine, bought from opposite Archie's college, rather than borrowed from the London Library opposite the home where they were soon to dwell in grief. In the Broad bicycles at a whizz were playing dodgems with the spaces between present and past. I did know that I was taking all this too hard and not taking it in at all. I was conjuring a spectral file of children in frilled frocks out of the Turl, parading them in front of my self-pity. I had the godlike advantage of pausing here in Tait's familiar street, staring at a Gothic structure that echoed his later Deanery in Carlisle, and pretending to experience with him, and with Catharine whom here in Oxford he had yet to meet, the death of a child whose conception was years off, buried in the womb of time. These were games played by the living in ignorance of the dead.

In irritation I turned against the way my mind worked and nearly got knocked down by a bike.

Two

In Wales an offer was made for our property. A speedy sale seemed imminent. With dread I drove back to our almost lost house to start closing it down. The insides were damply stacked with possessions. I stared into the old garden our many absences had let run wild. The leggy roses planted when the children were small were having a hard time thrusting beyond the reach of the nettles. A line of apple trees once as upright as a platoon had been variously blown out of true by the west winds that brought the soddening rain to Wales. The back garden on the slope had seen our hopes strangled by nature's prolixity. Into my mind, into my disappointment, came a whisper of a place in France we had visited only weeks ago.

We were visiting gardens in a minibus on a tour organised by a cousin of ours. Taking the ferry to and from Le Havre by night, we had basked in the unreal glow of spending one whole day abroad. Early on, in the hour before the crowds were let in, we were combing Monet's garden at Giverny for the originals of his landscapes. Everywhere you looked – at a bridge arching over pools of lilies, stonework awash with blossom – you saw a reality that lasted only a second pretending to be a painting that would last a lifetime. The model gardens were laid out in strips and squares of colour that confounded the palette by blushing or paling as the sun went in and out. Queues were already forming outside this open-air gallery that charged only a few francs for its masterpieces. Our exclusive party, having enjoyed sole rights for half an hour, moved on.

By noon, well away from the Seine, the minibus was probing deeper country. Every so often an aperitif passed out of reach as roadside cafés swept by. My tongue dried. At long last we parked in shadow at the start of a secluded drive.

The small group filed out eager for food and drink. But first a shock was in store. The trees in full leaf above our heads were curiously still. Not a sound breached the air. As we walked out of shadow into the beauty and breath of two thousand varieties of rose tightly packed into a modest acreage, the news spread among us in the hush that these gardens, hardly more than ten years old, were created in memory of Angélique, a daughter of the house who had died aged nineteen. Our garden would not otherwise exist. Appetite shrank.

The devoted gardeners, her parents, were still not far into middle age. They had planted their sorrow. They were letting their grief grow, expressing faith in the earth, bottling nothing up, working their muscles to the bone day after day, in and out of season, to draw sense and substance back into the world, in honour of some-one closer even than they were to each other: a child. A child, a celebration of love, a continuation of life: a future. Before I had been told in whispers a fraction of this story, as a glum chateau in miniature came into view behind the trees massed in their spring, my mind had turned back to the Taits. In the sunlight that now burned I was facing a scented mortuary open to the heavens.

The victuals were set out in a barn beside the gardens. Our cousin unloaded from hampers plenty of country pâté, watercress, tomatoes, and cheese. We tucked in with that freedom from manners licensed by picnics. Bottles of a heavy wine lightened the mood. We quaffed to an excess permitted by being not at home. It felt little different from a wake; the intoxicating effect of the gardens in such bloom was to bring Angélique back to life. Very nearly she was helping her parents with the *tarte aux pommes* they were now serving with coffee as a compliment to our party's visit. Her father gave me a slice of the tart and dolloped on to it the rich local cream as yellow as the rose that dangled over the window in an irrepressible climb up the house to the rooftops. On the last swig of wine, before we were summoned once more into the garden, hazes of scent assaulting the air, a white clematis climbing theatrically into the midst of a crab-apple tree, some varieties of rose fading, some dropping, others only just in bud, it struck me anew that the blind and deaf adventure of living and dying was all simultaneous. I would not be here at all without Angélique or without death.

Some man was talking too loudly in the shadow of the trees as we trudged back in overall silence to the minibus. This male voice said Angélique's death had been recorded in *The Times*. With pride in his paradox he added that he considered her fate more tragic for the parents. I had seen him only minutes ago washing down slices of ham with half a litre of wine. His drunken tone told me that he meant what he was saying or knew what he was talking about.

Back to Portsmouth on the overnight ferry the hope of glimpsing Quarr Abbey stuck in my mind. But the dawn was too misty. And in London first enquiries at the newspaper drew a blank. Someone in features at *The Times*, when asked about a rose garden dedicated to the memory of a teenager, huffily responded as if I were accusing the press of failing to cover a great event. His know-all rasp from a busy desk was dispiriting. But remembering from France that man's vehemence, articulated through a mouth thick with wine, made me persist; he seemed to have felt in his heart what he had read in a paper. I took the risk of calling a chap I half knew at the *Telegraph* magazine: had they recently published anything about dead children? A day passed. Then purring into my machine came a darkly faxed account, over several pages, of a tragedy.

That fellow swaying among the riotous hybrids on the way out of the picnic lunch in Normandy had got it wrong, but right. He had recalled, not Angélique, who had died, but Geneviève, who had suffered a death. Two deaths. The death of two daughters under the age of ten – and I shivered; she called it *La Disparition*. For she had followed Catharine Tait into print. She had updated mourning for daughters. She had dragged disappearance into today, and it was still the same: helpless, timeless, hopeless. The few columns in the *Telegraph* were extracted from a book, a book forced out of her, upon her, a book she never wanted to write, just as Catharine had sat down at Hallsteads and tried too.

In the shop where I would later find Walter I now found Geneviève. On the inside flap of the jacket there she was, head wryly supported by her clenched fists, a smile half forced for the camera saddening her cheeks, her eyes a long way away.

I saw at once facts in my own life echoing hers off the page. We worked in capital cities; she lived in Paris, I in London. She too wrote for a living. Early in marriage she had given birth to two children, three years apart like ours. She had a home in southern France, a few miles from where I had lived when just her age; we used to use the same town. With even more resonance across a century did she echo Catharine in the stultifying fact of her loss. 'I immediately felt how impossible it was to raise myself to the scale of this event . . .' Nothing was coincidence; coincidence was an aspect of normality; all things were closer to everything else than we thought or were capable of thinking; that view did not disqualify us from supposing that everything too was random. 'The terror mounted in me out of all proportion to my own dimensions,' she said in the insurmountable wake of the news.

The two girls were being driven north-east on the motorway from Paris on a spring day. Their mother was at home, their father at work. Their aunt was at the wheel, her husband beside her, a baby strapped in. The two girls, Mathilde and Elise, were in the back on the way to their grandparents in The Hague for a royal celebration. A young driver passed too close, or skidded, it was by no means yet clear. ('I will tell you what happenened next, everything you want to know about what happened next, but at the moment I cannot.') For the moment it seemed a sidelong bump sent them into a swerve swiftly corrected, a wave of relief turning almost to smiles, then a quick glance into the back and the girls were gone. They were gone. They had been flung out on to the tarmac. 'I could not contain it all,' said Geneviève when the phone poured this news into her ear. 'It was expanding and expanding and I was not.' The girls were dead, cars only just missing them, passing at speed, and the facts went into slow motion. 'I was still this little woman in her little apartment, next to a little man in the same little apartment. The terror targeted us exclusively, we were its only prey, its only destination, the terminus; it was a giant and we were dwarves. Laurent took me by the wrists and asked me not to scream. He said: "To think we're going to have to get over this."

'A big part of us has stayed there for ever.'

I went on reading as I walked homeward, avoiding ('the moment in life we do not all experience') news-stands just in time, sidestepping ('the moment when something takes aim at us') the phalanxes of tourists massed on the grubby pavement, walking in the gutter as taxis slipped and streamed past my hearing.

Trying to avoid the chaos of Piccadilly Circus, she was pitching her words above the asphyxiating pound of the traffic; 'Mathilde and Elise left at exactly the right moment for [him] to kill them, them and only them. In order for this to happen, there was an extraordinary accumulation of concordant circumstances. If just one of them had been omitted, no one would have known what sort of disaster we had escaped . . .' I crossed Haymarket at a dance between red buses to drab buildings that had long since buried the old arcades that fed and watered Walter's concupiscence. Every day we were escaping death because a single detail of the equation had failed to click into place: a change of gear, a foot on the brake, one gulp of wine more or less, the door shutting at home only at the second attempt, someone bumping into me to cause a second of delay.

Turning towards St James's Square, where thoughts of the Taits lay in leafy ambush, I took Geneviève into the well-preserved Victorian pub opposite Apple Tree Yard and over a glass of wine mused on the total lack of coincidence in living close to her in France. In the early 1970s I had thought Uzès a paradise which later veered towards a hell. I inhabited a farmhouse outside the town; so, on the way to mine, did Geneviève and her husband. At weekends she commuted from Paris. 'Then on the plane I think about him and the children and the little path behind the house lined with brambles where the two of us used to walk at night in the first few summers,' she said, and I remembered actually seeing their house every Saturday as I drove into that centre of the Middle Ages to shop: our city in miniature was densely enclosed within a circle of boulevard, once the defensive wall and now strung with cafés under overarching plane trees, and Geneviève would surely be there. Every Saturday the street market descended in vans and trailers from all over the region to pack with stalls every medieval crevice of an alley, heaping the Place aux Herbes at the town's heart with mounds of olives matt green and shining black, quicksilver swathes of fish glittering under the eye, cheeses from every ripe corner of France arrayed on the mobile counters, cases of fruits piled from the wider Provence at our doorstep, thickets of herbs to flavour the week to come, vegetables picked fresh that dawn from the valleys where our houses lay: all this proliferation swaddling us, all this life spoiling us, death having assaulted only the past.

I must have seen her. The cafés were busy and young. Strong sunlight filtered by leaves played through the wine on to the table top. A slight breeze often tempered the heat. Couples like these Jurgensens sat sipping the idleness of noon, before the whole of the Midi paused lengthily for lunch. Amid the youth assembled in chat at a diminishing perspective of tables down the boulevard, she and Laurent had just got married. Very soon, one August holiday melting the ice too fast in the pastis, they were here with the infant Mathilde, born in 1973, a year before I finally left the outdoor cafés to be occupied by others.

A big part of us has stayed there for ever.

Geneviève's account of the deaths, shorter than Catharine Tait's essay but taking her a decade longer to write, described in detail her total failure to recover even by writing. As with Catharine, other babies were born to Geneviève. Two, in due course; a girl, then a boy. They were children so touched by parental grief that they sensibly grew to regard their two sisters as still part of the family.

Geneviève's story was told in letters to a close male friend and told wobblingly, at intervals, when she felt she had controlled her feelings enough to be able to get words down without their going runny. I leaned at the bar reflecting that I had bought her book in fear of being bowled over by her horribly incidental discovery that the key to life, and the grip of mockery life held us in, was death: death, second only to birth, the grinning brackets at each end of life's little phrase; and as with Catharine I felt impelled to read fast while unable to bear reading other than slowly. And what Geneviève found out about tragedy was: 'The reality remains inaccessible.' She was dogged by the 'same feeling of shallowness' when she talked of a daughter's death as when capturing in a snapshot one of their living successors. She observed: 'The love that nourished your happiness will nourish your pain.' She asked: 'Does anyone ever really confront the contradiction between life and death? Often I felt their life was so powerful that I would tell myself that they could not be dead; but just as often their absence seemed so complete that I no longer believed I had known them.'

Meanwhile they moved about ground long hallowed in my pantheon of place. They had supper at a friend's house near the Pont du Gard. They played tennis in Uzès against the fringe of shaggy hills among which I lived. Their Paris had scraps of my adolescence buried in it. With ease my eye followed them out of the city towards a church in Compiègne – not far from the railway carriage that signed an armistice in 1919 and a defeat in 1940 – where the joint funeral of the girls took place: an event, for these parents, hardly less charged with inexpressible grief than that pair of cataclysmic wars.

Here at the Welsh house we were selling, Geneviève's pages lay open on a table piled with cork mats, electrical wiring, a relief map of the area, bath salts, a tie, some notebooks, an ashtray from the oyster bar at Bentley's – detritus of a family life thrown into irremediable chaos by moving on. Before the funeral of Mathilde and Elise, said Geneviève, someone 'sat next to me and said something that I did not understand, that I still do not understand today. But at that moment I knew that in the mystery and truth of her affirmation there was great vision. She said: "They did have a full life all the same." I know that one day, before I die, I will understand this sentence. I know that it is above reason and that in order to assimilate it I have to reach a dimension which is not yet part of me . . .'

I reread this sentence quietly in Wales. At this point in the pub I had snapped the book shut and, feeling omnidimensional, moved out into this immemorially multi-layered quarter of London. St James's Square lured me as ever, a vertical palimpsest of aged trees aligning with older houses. Just to make sure in the interest of accurate research that Tait's episcopal town house really had succumbed to one of the capital's periodic rashes of redevelopment, I had emerged from the gardens to confront its site on the south-east of the square, and lo! a classical frontage in yellow brick with window facings of white stone reared out of the concrete neighbours squeezing it tight on both sides. On a discreet plaque the building was marked 'London House'.

The place was closed. But within I glimpsed a curve of stairway rising with grace behind a janitor in immaculate uniform. I touched the bell in an appeal for admittance to a time I had thought gone. As briskly as a footman he rose to answer the summons. Yes, indeed, this was where bishops of London had lived; inside I might find much changed, but not all, and I was welcome to apply to the company to pay the house a visit. Closing the door, he retired courteously into the nineteenth century.

As I stared at the outside, a maid bustled up from the area on some errand. At once Walter appeared to enter St James's Square on a wet night gazing in passing at the lit windows of the bishop whose charity he supported, only to be distracted by the lure of a servile female hurrying into the dark. Of such commotion in his trousers Walter had recorded dozens of instances; his eleven original volumes amounted to 4200 pages, if not longer than the Bible, no less repetitive. From youth onward Walter had 'kept a diary of some sort', which now and then he fed from memory. Archie's diaries were an outline of his previous week; as his biographer put it, 'to arrange his thoughts, whether about work, or politics, or books, or travel, or devotion, in what he called an "adhesive" shape'. Always Walter followed the girl, and described what he did to her, just as Archie always followed the truth, and described how he dealt with it. Each was confined within the limits of his own confessional. Each preached good news.

'The oldest incidents I am convinced are taking place daily everywhere, between men and women, who are, or who are going to, or have been fucking on the sly, but of which the world can know nothing,' said Walter from the pulpit of his prose. 'I suppose such risks really add to our enjoyment. Such are my conclusions, after the experience of nearly a quarter of a century of intriguing and fucking women, including all classes, from a marchioness to well-nigh a beggar.'

'Our three little girls very engaging,' scribbled Tait six years into his London appointment. 'Baby has taken to insisting on saying her little prayer to me before she goes to bed. Little Edith came to us on the sands, saying, "God can't see me, can He? He is in Heaven; how can He? He can't see me when I am in bed. Where is He then?" It was the continuation of an argument with Lucy. I repeated to her the words of her hymn about "One I cannot see who loves and cares for me".'

'How grateful I am to my Creator', Walter went on, 'that he has thus far made me better and wiser than the beasts of the field, to whom the heavenly delights of gamahuching and minetting are unknown. It is in such delicious, voluptuous pastimes that man is superior to other animals on the globe. To lick such a lovely cunt and give delight to its possessor is a sign of the divinity which lives, whilst I live, within me.'

'If I could tell you the story of our grief,' Tait wrote from Hallsteads, 'you would see what a call we have to look upon this world as the merest pilgrimage. But all these softening and holy impressions may in time wear away through the pressure of business and the deep interest of the continued cycle of great employments that seems to be before me.'

To the rear of my mind their voices coincided. Neither questioned the other's premises or differed from his conclusions. The thought which had shamed me earlier in the search, that they were one and the same Victorian gentleman, varying not even in degrees of honesty, refused to go away. The notion that a man felt as guilty when he worshipped a capricious god as when he rogered a married woman vibrated through their combined pages, and edged me into despair of faith in anything, except the blazing lucidity of death.

Meanwhile here in Wales I awaited confirmation of the sale of our home: the signal to close down a paradise and pack up twenty years of mess. When I arrived yesterday in an inferno of perfect weather I fell into my usual gloom at failing to coincide at once with the place's shy nature. Hours of pounding down the motorway still echoed in my ears. And the farmers from the next valley who were supposed to be buying the place had already moved in the tractors, grinding up and down the next field where an untidy length of hawthorn hedge had been uprooted. The noise choked a whole afternoon with dust.

The night was troubled with dreams, which sprang me awake, fizzling out. Again I pursued that idea of dreams as the link that joined us all, a link more vivid (like faith) than normal communication (like talk). Yet we denied memories of dreams to ourselves (for fear of truth) and to others (for fear of boring). But suppose I thought of dreams as a means of striking through to the eternal, an idea so far beyond belief (like faith) that it had the power to swamp the spirit and extinguish doubt in the mind? So, on this take, dreams were a connection to another world. If you chose to regard them as the trash of your unconscious, your mind's daily dollop of excretion, that was your affair; you ran the awful risk of limiting yourself. It came to me in bed that the agony the Taits suffered was still in existence, not just in the actual experience of those now alive like Geneviève, but in the archival forms their dreams turned into, a language into which (if only I knew what key to touch) I might one day tune. I knew this to be beyond reach, of course, to brains as ill-developed as mine; but it remained a metaphor for faith as moving as the thing itself was, to those it touched.

At dawn I rang the farmer to ask if he would mind calling off the tractors. The rest of the day I was caught up in the buzzing summer bliss, insects emphasising the silence as they whizzed in and out of it. I was in my proper element, as soundless as owl flight or the look of deep water. I dozed in the heat, and the dreams came and went, untroubled now, forming stories that at once slid out of the mind. Now and then a distant dog barked into them. A far-off train rattled them. The dreams were concerned with loss. Again I wondered where they had gone; again I felt I was on the tantalising point of finding out. But that feeling too like a dream kept sliding.

We had bought Wales largely for its isolation. It was three miles beyond and above a market town. The house stood wrapped in the privacy which our rambling surround of thirty acres secured for it. In the swells of a huge green view other dwellings were pinpoints of whitewash far away, on more than one undulant horizon. If in sight at all, someone else's residence seemed to exist across a border, in another country. Up here at home I was in a land of my own. It made me feel invisible. Yet I doubted if even here I could gather the audacity of mind to find a faith for myself, with only a month of ownership left.

Part IV

One

On my way to lunch with someone at the Garrick Club a few days later I stepped into Waterstone's to see if I could lay hands on *My Secret Life* without having to ask an assistant. The book was not (or not much) of 'gay interest'; yet there seemed no special section for us straights. I twice passed a small revolving bookcase in mid-floor before realising that I had missed the run of salacious titles merely because they were below eye level rather than (as in newsagents) above it. Sure enough, packed between classics of whip and leather, Walter's three paperbacks occupied a respectable four inches of shelf.

With a hot pride in buying for the first time in my life thousands of pages of unrepentant sex, I bore them to the counter where without a flicker a young woman totted them up and processed my card. The three covers were voluptuously adorned by nudes reclining alone in bed. Out in the street, with only yards to stroll to the club, I slipped one volume half out of the paper bag and half opened it at random. '. . . and grasped her smooth fat buttocks,' I read. 'I have no sense of time, all is oblivion and elysium . . . Our sighs of pleasure are over . . .' and I had reached the foot of the Garrick steps.

I gave my name, the porter bent courteously forward as if to relieve me of my books, yes, my host was in the bar, yes, I could leave my package safely in the cloakroom. The brown paper was slightly torn where in haste I had stuffed the smooth fat buttocks back into the bag. From the book's spine a naked breast showed through the rip. As a prize-winning biographer moved past with a nod on his way to the lavatory, I tried to repack my parcel respectably. A former cabinet minister hung up his overcoat. But again scraps of sentence drew my eye. 'Going one Saturday night up Granby Street, Waterloo Road, then full of women who used to sit at the windows half-naked . . . Upon her saying "Come and have me," replied that I had scarcely any money. "Never mind," said she, "we will have a fuck for all that" . . .' Not far from Lambeth Palace, I thought academically, hoping I would now meet a bishop washing his hands. But only the biographer was vainly mirrored combing his thin hair and, without knowing each other, we exchanged a pleasantry in good club style.

No less stylish and polite, while consulting the menu, my host expressed interest in what I was doing with my life, so while partly thinking of the fuse of Walter's time bomb sizzling among the behatted pegs below, I talked about Catharine Tait, and how much I felt drawn to her. A senior clergyman ushered himself into the dining room and sat next to the biographer. In a whisper more intense than embarrassed I now quoted Catharine in her own voice. 'I was alone in bed, and there came to me a feeling of agony and terror . . .' My friend was impressed, fawningly comparing my few words of hers to the memorising of a love letter. A liveried sleeve loomed, a gentle wrist poured claret into my glass with hardly a gurgle. In this room, or one like it, where Tait must have been lunched and Walter entertained, I was feeling somewhere between honoured by my setting and humoured by my host: a limbo that needed a drink. I started telling him, as lamb cutlets were served on to a plate too hot to touch, how when the third daughter died and the other three children were exiled from the Deanery to protect their health, Catharine had a vision. A vision! Leaning across the comestibles, my friend looked as sincere as a man might when stricken by belief. A vision? Well, it was not quite a dream, for she was awake. Nor was it a revelation, for she instantly felt deluded by it. Somewhere in the house lay her baby Lucy. 'All seemed going from us,' Catharine said, 'and at once. I was above their schoolroom, from which, a few days before, I used to hear the happy, merry voices. Now I heard distinctly a sound of terror. A loud distinct swell from the notes of their piano, and immediately after the little voices seemed calling "Papa! Papa!" I knew it was not so, yet distinctly I heard it, and, jumping out of bed, ran to my Husband. He could not come . . .'

I helped myself to more redcurrant jelly. I found the meat drily difficult to get down; my swallow had got stuck on the words.

Abruptly my host asked if I had ever been in love. Was it not like faith?

And I was suddenly opening my arms to a woman I once knew for a spell. I had not thought of her, I told my host, for a quarter of a century. I had been susceptible to her existence on earth for only a few days. I saw her in Stockholm not more than twice or three times: golden times on a knife edge of the divine. To this day I viewed her as a visitation I had let slip.

I met her through a figure who had been or still was her lover. My first clothed image of her was belly down, legs idly kicking, on the wooden floor of his lowlit apartment somewhere in the city. The inexact location was to be part of the lure in memory. Uncertain of space as of time, I was shaken by the instantly erotic sense that I was going to be converted to her, without knowing who or what she was, but trusting in her; it was enough that my close friend had tasted her. I had, or preferred to have, little recall of how we, independently of him, made contact thereafter. But a meeting was bound to occur. I cadged her number or she sneaked mine. Married to someone never mentioned, she lived in a grey stately block in a loftier section of town. After I had done all I could to evade her, she was to descend on my borrowed flat, with an inevitability as potent as permanence.

First she offered me a whole weekend to plunder, and in a panic trembling with sex, fearful of hopeless commitment, I arranged for myself a safe passage to Helsinki on the overnight boat secure in the company of two women who loved each other. I left the country without calling her. I took off, I drank and danced, I marked time, almost hoping that on our return a night later to Stockholm it would be too late. I feared her shy boldness. Fighting excitement, mind battling against instinct, I despaired of what wrenching changes I might be forced by the power of her breath and body to make to my serenity. When at last we snatched up the phone, a taxi ride apart, time had shrunk in availability to one long black night, I soon had to catch a train elsewhere, servicing lesser urges and aims. Her voice was slushy with desire, no more to be resisted than mine in husky reply. In an hour or so? No, please, sooner, as near to now as possible. It was as if the instrument at our mouths and ears had been invented for this last-minute act of blind faith. Our voices were running away together.

Her body was on its way to me. I dashed down to the street, time too short to lose, to buy in all sorts of fish, smoked, marinated, slivers of eel, salmon thinly sliced, herring in mustard or dill sauces swimming in vinegar sweetened by onion, assortments of salad in handfuls, bread in plump brown loaves or crisp white lengths, white wine by the bottle and lashings of red, for this first and last supper, before I rattled back on the rails to the normality I no longer desired. The flat lent me was in the old town, two storeys up through a cobbled courtyard, and in that shadowy enclave, on time, I heard her cab door slam shut, a step on the cobbles, the ring at the bell, and then my open door, the vestibule dim: she taller than I remembered, her eyes on mine, thigh-high black boots she at once bent to zip off as though at home, long slim legs in black, striding here and there half on tiptoe urgently to explore the spaces and opportunities of the flat. Her ranginess was both creating appetite and controlling it. Soon she sat opposite me at table, pouring with a familiar hand the white wine I had opened. She was given not to seduction but to truth. She knew we knew what we were here for: simply love, its limitless chances, its twin power to enslave and liberate, its third to hurt.

After our supper, hand in hand with slopping glasses of wine, we spent a long spell, as the small hours grew, making half-love with deepening arousal on chair, sofa, halfway to floor, lamplight penetrating from the street, her mouth openly softening, her heart beating against me beneath her swell of breast, her smooth buttocks under my hands. We sat askew to each other, making the best of our bodies without giving them up to each other, wrapped in the ease and awkwardness of each other's arms, playing at love without making it. Even beyond the eleventh hour towards dawn, when we were naked, I was unable to relax my grip on disbelief. No power on earth or in heaven could make me give myself to her or take her.

Going slowly southward after that overdose of brevity, I was conscious of her presence in the train across Provence and northern Italy on the way to Venice; in Venice seeming to sit with her or her shadow in the shade drinking a negroni in the Piazza San Marco or straining my eyes at a tearful fresco; looking for her or her double on the ship that loitered down the Adriatic through the tricks of the sun on the wine-dark water. We bypassed Ithaca apart and together. In Athens, traipsing up the Acropolis with only her image in tandem with my solitude, I wanted to send this woman in Stockholm a secret communication which no practical difficulty must thwart. Better than a letter from me, higher than a poem by anyone, bigger than the distance between us, something unimaginable that existed – a prayer to a goddess: I thought of a Beethoven quartet.

With little cash or time to spare, on the run from a marriage in which I could no longer breathe or believe, I wrote out a cheque to a department store in central Stockholm. Of no fixed address, without knowing or wanting to know the cost of a quartet or who might have recorded it, I posted off a garbled instruction into the blue: please send a message of belief in civilisation (Op 18, No 1) to someone I had just started loving; and would never have the courage to throw myself at the feet of, and doted on the mouth of, the heavenly smile that made the eyes roll and the heart leap.

Even in making it I knew this arrangement lacked, like any overture of sex, certainty. Yet, sex being omnipotent, I trusted: she would be converted by the tone and tunes of the quartet to the underlying passion, which struck me as having most of Europe in it, plenty of history, not to mention fun, plus a feel of eternity and something upliftingly beyond it; all life bled out of that music. Poking my head in and out of noisy joints on the Plaka, muddled on cheap retsina, I viewed this gift of a quartet as biblical in power, a gospel uniting us in absence.

I never knew what effect the disc had, even if it arrived. We never met again or spoke or corresponded. Later I wondered if the woman, in that so short revelation, was the only person I was ever in love with; and loved still, the mystery irresoluble. My room near Omonia Square had a balcony on which I sat foolishly at noon in a sweat, drinking. From the flower market below I had bought a potted bougainvillea, voluminously blooming as bright as splashes of blood, to be passed on to the person unknown who stayed here next. But I thought only of my woman; of the one night, she half out of her clothes with lascivious mischief, I half out of my mind with guilt, when she again and again urged honesty upon me.

In Athens, trying to send her music, worshipping from afar, I saw in the heat that I had missed faith by inches. Leaning over the balcony I felt sickened by the wasted chance. I had failed to embrace the opportunity she offered, the heights she promised, the person she was. All along she had been speaking a different language from mine, as total in hope and force as the music I was trying to send.

At the Garrick, by the time I had got this story off my chest, having finished the claret, we had succumbed to port. All over London a hazy afternoon was slipping between the sheets in borrowed rooms or hotels in side streets long emptied of chic. I wished I had a few hours of such seamy siesta over again. Out here in Floral Street, as I tripped at the kerb, the torn bag deposited a volume of Walter into the gutter. It fell open at no particular place. But bending down to wipe sludge off the page edges I caught a sentence of Walter at the top of his form. Even on all fours in a public street I could hardly ignore the few words I was wiping off with my handkerchief. 'During the next four days,' Walter was saying about a maid called Bates, 'I fucked her on the table in the dining room, in the arbour, in my bedroom, and on Sunday night up against a tree in a lane on her way to church. She did really go to church but with my spunk in her cunt, and only just before service was over.'

Snatching the book up off the tarmac, I saw the back entrance of Stanford's map shop. Yes, I knew what love and loss were. They were drawn from the same source. They drew their pain from sex. 'We who know so little the beginning or the end of all things instead of calling the sexual organs and their conjunction foul and obscene,' Walter was saying, 'should rather sing loud paeans in praise of them, for they are emblems of the Creator, fucking is obedience to his laws, and is worship of him.' True, but not enough: we had to mature beyond the gentrification of smut. Just in time I remembered that they sold maps reprinted from the past in this shop. Hallsteads was marked on one I had briefly seen. I could also get a plastic bag to replace the torn brown paper only just covering the three volumes of *My Secret Life* which kept slipping out of a hand loosened by one glass of port too many.

I bought the first edition from the 1860s of the one-inch Ordnance Survey which had Hallsteads on it. I also found that the original Stanford himself had mapped London with exactitude in 1862, and his black-and-white plans of street and river and park, page after page of them, bound into a floppy volume, looked more vital than any reality imaginable. With a magnifying glass, when I unfolded this treasure at home, I imposed on the etching a minute image of Walter sneaking with libidinous eye up and down alleys long since demolished in futile efforts to cleanse the city of vice. I saw too the rooftops of the bishop's residence in St James's Square, beneath which Catharine's inability to play the tragedy queen, and Tait's capacity to maintain a rational front, anaesthetised them enough from loss to begin copulating towards a future.

Two

Not long after that lunch at the Garrick, I was travelling north to Carlisle by train, at last to visit the Deanery. To read on the journey, and properly to face for the first time, I was carrying Catharine Tait's account of the deaths of her daughters. In my raincoat pocket I had Volume II of 'Walter' for relief. I flicked open a page where Walter too was on a train. He had a memorable gift for trailers. The present shorthand, written at roughly the time when the Taits were moving to Fulham Palace, ran thus: 'At Aldershot. – The postage stamp. – The Major's mistress. – The Railway carriage. – Carnal hints. – Carnal practice. – A pretty foot. – At the garters. – Head near tail. – A seductive priapus. – Upon the floor. – Upon the seat.' The full story hardly needed to be told.

My back to the engine so that town and suburb slipped out of sight in front of me, we gathered speed through the tunnel beneath Primrose Hill. As I tried to find my place in Catharine's book, my eye fell on this puzzle of a sentence. 'Before that day came,' Catharine wrote, 'we had to learn a solemn lesson, that we cannot choose the circumstances of our grief.' I turned a page or two. It was no good pretending that I was on my way to faith. But at least I had a clearer idea of why I lacked it, thus perhaps of what it was: a pulling of the wool over your own eyes as necessary and narcotic as drink or fags or drugs or any other of the illusion manufacturers by which life forced us to live.

My eye lapsed. The brain fogged into disjointed images. Vaguely I was seeing myself as a man raped by worship secretly conjoined with sex; disappointed rather than traumatised by that mixture; always on the brink of gloom but never maturing enough for depression: envious of those more ennobled by hurt than myself. Tait, travelling north towards his young family after the fatigue of a London conference, nodded off in his seat, the pulse of steel wheels echoing off sleepers hard on the ears. As the motion lulled me too I wondered whether in Tait's case, or equally in mine, the best sketch of paradise might be outlined in dreams. They sprang from life; they were a usefully scrambled version of it; but nobody had yet explained where they went, into what super-astral archive. For dreams had an air of permanence, an authority, which their raw material badly lacked. They behaved as if they meant business. They treated us humans as if they were manipulating us for their own never-stated purpose.

I was shaken awake when we were passing at reduced speed through the cavern of Rugby station. Colleagues in the church were to say that Tait's spell at Rugby was the happiest time of his life. He had intimates to stay. He entertained generously. All shades of opinion were welcomed into the candlelight of his drawing room. He took long walks and longer rides. He cared for the boys. Yet later lore had it that, as headmaster of a public school, Tait failed.

The problem was Dr Arnold, jealously lauded as a genius by the loyal staff Tait inherited. That Tait was not 'a finished scholar' earned him stick, though he was commended for his tact in dealing with men. Controversy got him into hot water within the church both high and low, but served only to confirm him in a lifelong fight against extremes: an advocate of good sense thanks to good humour. 'I mistrust an enthusiast,' he used to say with a laugh, 'and all the more because I could never be one myself.'

Here at Rugby he suffered a sudden illness; a tendency to poor health lasted all his life. In March 1848 Catharine wrote to someone close to him, 'If you want to see your friend alive, come at once.' She had two babies by then, Catty and May; she was cool and brief, as if already organised for death.

By Ash Wednesday in 1848, that famous year of revolutions across the Continent, Tait was indeed at death's door from rheumatic fever. Only when he was slightly on the mend weeks later did the school follow Europe's example: the boys too broke into noisy rebellion. The uprising was quelled, the hubbub quieted, by rising murmurs of 'Tait, Tait!' The thought of their hero in his sick room overhearing their mob outburst provided, as an old boy put it, 'an instant sedative'.

Only by full summer was Tait fit enough to emerge from seclusion. By way of recuperation he attended a cricket match in the Close on a warm day when 'his stately form was seen, supported by Mrs Tait, walking under the elms'. Bats were dropped, balls thrown aside, amid cheers that welcomed him back into the heart of the school. 'He was always rather the statesman than the schoolmaster,' wrote his pupil Arthur Butler, 'the ruler than the friend. But . . . we had been drawn to him in his illness; we understood him better. We felt . . . what a depth of passionate emotion lived under that calm and dignified exterior. And when the time came, two years after, for him to remove to Carlisle, the flood of loyalty and affection rose to its height.'

On the day of his departure several boys including Butler took over from the horses and dragged his carriage to the station. As the train puffed away northwards, one boy thought what an odd way to show regret, as though they were glad to be rid of him. Another wondered what he would have thought of it himself. A third suggested, quoting Tait's own formula, 'There is a good deal to be said on both sides.' Whereupon one of them asked, 'How shall we ever get on without him?' – 'With which boylike mixture of jest and earnest', Butler concluded, 'of criticism and affection, we took leave of our old Headmaster.' Old was a relative or fond term. On his first journey by rail to Carlisle the new Dean was thirty-eight.

In the book on my lap Catharine was now writing after the first death, 'Just then there rushed to my heart a feeling of separation from them which I could not bear, and an intense faintness.' Her text often melted into these spasms, her prose so much a mistress of the distressful that I kept involuntarily averting my head from the page. To try reading beyond 'I went to my own room, and got ready to have our last look at that little form which was that night to be closed from mortal sight' took an effort beyond words.

Again in the train north my eyes dimmed. More than half asleep, not quite half awake, I could hear her voicing words I had read just before sliding into this haze. 'What was coming? New trial, that I felt sure of – more separation. Was I, by a sudden stroke, to be taken and they left? It seemed to me likely to be so that

Sunday; its hours passed solemnly, as I walked about the passage leaning on my husband's arm, or lay on the sofa, unable to fix my thoughts.' The signboards for a station, probably Stafford, whipped past the eye too fast to be sure.

Again I found myself compulsively rereading an earlier death in an effort to make it real. At the Deanery Chatty's funeral was set for tomorrow: 'Towards evening I again felt very faint,' said Catharine, 'and with a feeling of exceeding dread upon me . . . Meantime I went to sleep, and awoke in the morning at first feeling well, but in a few minutes the faintness and the dread returned again. It was the morning of my Chatty's funeral. I felt I dare not go.'

As the train drew slowly through Crewe came the shock more bizarre than unexpected. 'It will be too cold for you to go,' the doctor said, 'and I think the children had better not.' Before Catharine had time to reply, he said, 'Do you know the child Susan is ill?' The train whirling me backwards through unknown countryside, Catharine went on, 'I said, "No; is it fever?" He said, "I fear it is." At once I felt quite well myself, and this came like light to my mind, "We are in God's hands." '

Like light to my mind. Never had I been pulled so hard awake by someone's faith. To her it was almost a relief, a confirmation of worst fears, that the small daughter who had the wrong wreath put on her head, and climbed into the empty seat, was on the very day of her sister's funeral doomed. I knew what Catharine meant: it was all meant. The fight went out of her. The resignation entered in triumph. She stood, sensing it but without believing it, on the edge of the meaningless.

I closed the book on the folding table and swayed off

to the rear of the train to add light to my mind with a
gin and tonic. Given time, the second gin and tonic
would take the edge off the meaninglessness. Speeded
by alcohol, tracts of England flew by. Fifty years ago I
had been conveyed up this railway at public expense to
join the RAF at Warrington, our next stop. A. C. Tait
had used the line not long after steam locomotives first
reached as far north as Carlisle.

Swigging my drink, I recollected that Walter too was
travelling by train when on the platform at Aldershot
he encountered a major's wife who wanted a postage
stamp for a letter. 'She handed it to me and I put on the
stamp. "Wait, guard, a second only" – and I rushed to
the station master who just then appeared, and gave it
him, turned back, saw the lady looking anxiously out of
a first-class carriage, jumped into it with her, winking
at the guard, who locked the door, and almost before I
was seated, the train went off. It was an express to
Waterloo.'

Opposite me at a diagonal sat a woman who looked
ghostly in the darkening reflection of the window.

'You must give me a kiss for my postage stamp.'
Walter had a relentless line in the suggestive, wasting
no time on small talk. 'I got as close to her as the arm
between the seats (a fixture) allowed. My leg met hers,
and she didn't move it away. Carelessly I laid my hand
on her knee, and, pinching up a bit of the silk dress,
admired it. Now every second she looked at me, and
then out of the window, then at me again, and I saw in
her eyes voluptuous wants . . .'

Outside, remnants of the industrial revolution slipped
by: factories, turned into warehouses, transformed into
leisure centres, occupying the core of towns which the

train rushed past. The woman across was caught suddenly in the glass staring into a glow of sunset.

'Coquettishly she put one foot on the opposite seat, I stopped, and had my hands on her thighs in a second . . . "Now leave me alone – Oho – don't – do leave off – we shall be seen." We whisked past a station. "Oh, if my husband knew, I should be ruined for life – oh – I *will* dine with you then, and you *shall* after dinner," and her backside and thighs moved with . . . that restless wriggling of belly, buttocks . . . that a woman can't help giving when . . . the luscious sensation of complete lewdness, and the want of fucking, are coursing through her body . . .

'I saw victory before me now,' Walter went on. 'I rose standing before her, my prick almost touching her face, as she sat with her eyes fixed on it, whilst I begged her. "I won't. I can't lie down on the floor." "Take off your bonnet then and sit where you are." She did. I put cushion after cushion on the floor, to bring myself to a convenient height, then, kneeling down, I opened her thighs, threw up her petticoats . . . We looked in each other's faces till our eyes closed in the swooning pleasure of the crisis . . . Then we sat and talked. "It was awfully quickly over." "It was – where is my bonnet? That's the consequence of asking for a postage stamp," said she. "Lucky for me," I replied.'

The sun finally sank in time to the last gulp of gin. Somewhere out there in the gloom lay Hallsteads, where I caught Catharine at another bad pass: 'I got up and went to my window, and saw the little coffin carried out. In heart and mind I followed, but not in body; joined in the silence of my own chamber in that solemn Service, and then strove to realise the gain for my beloved lamb, and sought for strength for what might yet be before us.' The doctor came, 'looked at my Susan, and said, "That child is doing very well; she could not have it better."' An hour later she was 'in a fit . . . It had come in a moment, and, after Chatty's case, hope left us at once. Everything that man could do was done . . . The little lovely one lay unconscious . . . The little body was quite stiff, the arms and legs twitching, the eyes open, but no sight for anything more in this world . . . At five o'clock Mrs Peach took her again, and I, feeling very ill, went to my own room and lay down. At seven, her Father came to tell me he thought our darling would not be with us many more minutes. I rose in haste, and went with him. It was a sight full of agony; the conflict with death was long. Between six and seven more hours we kept our sad watch, expecting every moment that all would be over . . . She died on Thursday, March 11th, and in sadness and bitterness of heart we went together to the drawing-room and sat there. I never saw my little lamb again.'

Doors slammed close to my ear. I had lost touch with the outside. Oxenholme? Or Penrith? Somewhere within the night Catharine was bent over the grim duty of her account at Hallsteads, the words drying as her moving hand covered a page: that was the reality. I was still outside it, confined in the long airless box of the train.

With the carriages grinding over the points into Carlisle station, I quickly took in a couple more of Catharine's sentences. 'Our schoolroom, the three we had brought with us to Carlisle, were still with us, and we knew what a treasure we had in them. We looked sadly on our little Frances as we felt that one on each side of her was gone; still, she was very bright, too young to miss them, and baby was given to take, as it were, little Susan's place on earth, and we could think calmly, though sadly, of those two sweet ones bearing each other company in the kingdom of their Saviour in heaven, and perhaps watching over the beloved ones they had left.'

At the station I was met. My family gathered around me. I would soon be lapped in comforts that would put the Taits at a decent remove. Full of chat, we drove out of the city, street lamps diminishing in rear-view mirrors, crossing the bridge over the Eden, which had borne the weight of the funerals. Up to the right on an unseeable knoll stood the church at Stanwix, enclosing in its yard the five-sided monument to the girls. In the melodramatic dark I pictured it surrounded by lesser tombstones, half fallen or cracked, the mortality of the nineteenth century petrified in a dance of death. Tomorrow I would view the scene, if it had not passed beyond decay.

At my wife's family home to the north of Carlisle the presence of Catharine lay in wait for me. Unavoidably she would drop in after supper as if I had invited her. I knew what fate had in store, but the mind, as hers did, still refused it. 'Sweet Susan, who had taken Chatty's place the Sunday before, had since Tuesday been with her in heaven,' she said matter-of-factly, 'and now, was Frances to follow? And how would it be with the others? All this our hearts began anxiously now to inquire.'

The reality and nearness of the world unseen.

I thought for a second that these words had arisen unprompted in me, but it was Tait who had uttered them: now they were true. Soon after eight o'clock we finished supper, the others retired into the half-dark to watch television, and without bothering to switch on lights in the passage I felt my way down to the garden room.

'About eight o'clock we were sitting by her,' said Catharine under the table lamp; 'she was worn out with fatigue, and kept saying to herself, "Oh, I am so tired! I am so tired!" Then I heard her say, as she fell off to sleep, "Our Father, which art in heaven."'

Meanwhile the doctor was called to the Deanery to examine the sleeping Frances. ' "Can you rouse her, and give her a little port wine?" . . . She made a great effort to take it, but said, "I can't, I can't" . . . I walked about the room in agony, not only because I knew now that this precious jewel must go, and that our home must ever miss this merry blessed little one, who had shed such brightness on it for four years – my will was subdued enough to feel that at our Father's call we could give up this one also – but we had jewels of untold value still untouched, and how I feared for them! A feeling was on my heart, "Is all this to prepare us for something much worse?" '

That night I dreamed as always, dreams here in the north, as in Wales, the more vivid for the country silence lapping at the ears. In the morning it occurred to me, as I pulled my socks on, that no longer was I in the normal way forgetting dreams. I was having them actively stolen. They did not just slip my mind. An invisible hand was palming them. In retrospect I had some evidence for this asinine revelation, I thought, as I caught a whiff of bacon frying downstairs. Years ago I had worked through a series of comic attempts to hang on to dreams at any cost. I tried to wrest them back from wherever they were escaping at full pelt. I determined to take notes on a spiral pad. At the time it hardly worried me that I knocked the pencil off the bedside table, overturned a glass of water, missed laying hands on my glasses, while the dream simply fled. I set the alarm to engineer interruption at some crucial moment in a dream – which then crumbled jaggedly in pains behind the eyes. But now, knotting my tie, sniffing breakfast below, I thought I knew different, I thought dreams had a strategy, I thought I must hang on to this thought before in the manner of a dream it faded to nothing.

After breakfast, when I was thinking of Catharine as if I had dreamed about her and all but forgotten, my father-in-law was on the telephone to the Dean. On the brink of retiring, the present incumbent was in the process of moving out of the Deanery. In instant response to a mention of A. C. Tait, he agreed to see us at two o'clock that afternoon.

As instructed we drove into the close and parked outside his front door in slow motion, among groups of tourists no less sluggish: I saw a funeral progress super-imposed on their aimlessness. In this holy territory I still felt at a loss. Behind the windows of the close facing one another on every side at odd angles too many places were hidden from me, places where without discovery a small boy might be unbuttoned or without hope a small girl deprived of health, neither girl nor boy within reach of the reason for the hugeness of what was assaulting them.

The Dean proved welcoming, clearheaded, helpful; he knew all about Tait. For the first time I felt I was not inventing my man, or my woman.

In the Deanery I had the sense of walking less on sacred than on scholarly ground, but all the same on tiptoe. I was stepping into presences: girls dying in the bewilderment of living among passages of parental grief. In the geography of the house the Dean's method was to establish the probable facts on the basis of likely assumptions. We looked into the strong chance that the hall windows on the ground floor were where the sick children in hasty isolation waved to their siblings, quarantined behind the windows of a house which stood the length of a cricket pitch opposite. Or was it from the landing upstairs that they gestured and blew kisses? Or, indeed, from this upper nursery, as one after another waving girl dropped plumb out of childhood into a black hole of eternity.

Like gossips we wafted about the Deanery in such lively speculation. I sensed a sharp division in the house between the Taits, husband and wife, he living studiously free at the tower end, she immured at the other with the children – together only when conceiving or burying them: a thought insupportable in these homely rooms.

A hotchpotch of a dwelling, altered, added to; the apartments had some grace but no grandeur. Bickley's description of the Deanery in his brief life of Tait as 'a curious, gloomy, rambling house' accorded with the photocopied engraving, from the *Gentleman's Magazine* of October 1811, which the Dean now gave me. It showed lower windows shrouded in shrubbery. The place was meaner before Tait himself added the good proportions of the room where we now sat discussing him. Beyond the churchy windows lay a lawn islanded between waves of flowers. The children had played in that safe compound. The Dean said that a door once led from this dining room to an outside lavatory sufficient to the needs of a whole household. The old front door, where the Taits welcomed and waved off their guests, the door through which the coffins with solemn frequency passed in and out empty or filled, had been suppressed. The old vestibule was now a utility room narrowing into a larder. Builders had helped wipe out the past. I felt distressed by this making good of a reality which I preferred to my own. It looked like botched attempts to paper over the truth.

The Dean used the word 'poignant' when talking of the Taits. Poignant too were the signs now, in this same house, of his own departure: rooms half packed up, heaps of bedding, cupboards gaping on ranks of empty hangers, unsteady piles of books waiting to be crated. Once again the house was on the edge of clearance. The rooms, halfway between one life and its unknown successor, were a mute echo of the agony that must quickly have swept the house clear of the immediate past in 1856, when the tenants could bear to spend no more time in it; and fled.

At moments, in different rooms, the phone rang, and the Dean left me alone for a minute or two. What might, indeed must, have happened in this or that room, their doors half open, flooded into me, the more swampingly for all these little signs of a family moving out. I could hear hurried conversations a room or two away as if they were voices from the wrong side of death. A train trundled over the viaduct. An insistent bell rang from the cathedral. In one of these intervals I saw a shift of curtains in the house opposite where the surviving children were isolated. It was a shiver, as of an invisible man yet again passing behind my life, taunting me enough to make my sex shrink: I was back in Hampshire, thirteen years old, feeling brave in an air raid, in a room with mullioned windows behind which I had been beckoned by the sub-organist for furtive reasons of his own.

In the quiet I felt the need to spend a night under this roof, to see what that would do to my dreams. I was surprised to find the place so alien, though I had no sense of the house being haunted. If anyone, it was I who was doing the haunting. I had brought my invisible man of old into it. I had let him loose and he had gone native in this paradise of young death.

And now the Dean hospitably returned and we were facing the landings where the girls last played and prayed as a family before the first blow struck.

Without ceremony the Dean produced keys, switched off a burglar alarm – and we stepped into a section of the Deanery long unused. In the upper chamber of the tower, Tait's study was huge, with views west over the railway arches that carried the acrid novelty of steam and speed, the cathedral rising to the east through tall windows, a fireplace wide enough to warm whole families for generations, leading the eye upward to a ceiling painted at a heady pitch of the Renaissance in 1520, criss-crossed by massive beams dividing those heraldic visions of this earthly life, to be viewed in all their magnificence only by cricking the neck. This was Tait's heaven. Here he sat back in reflection at the grand desk in his haunt of high-thinking privacy. Here he escaped the small crises that were the daily currency of family life beyond the door; but not the large ones.

I felt intrusive. The man was here. He was not here.

The Dean kindly took me through the detail of the pictorial history above our heads. Just cleaned of more than a century of railway smoke, the scenes were now as pristine as when Tait viewed them in reverie or anguish. All at once Tait seemed too hotly my contemporary. I was afraid of his version of the invisible man: the ghost who had done everything except appear.

Now and then in this house, when the Dean passed a window on the latch, the faintest of organ music mumbled on the air. But for the proximity of the cathedral my mind would have discounted it as memory. It lessened the invisibility of the people who no longer quite occupied these spaces. By the time we said goodbye on the doorstep the open air held no trace of it.

My father-in-law had other business in town, so I took Catharine's book out of the car and entered the cathedral, her words under my arm. There ahead stood the huge window which buried the little girls in the feverish hues of a symbolism best forgotten. Feet clattered down aisles as loud as furniture being moved. Tonelessly above me murmured a premonitory hiss which with a throb of pleasure I recognised. The organ was on hold, bellows full, awaiting another set of blind instructions from someone's fingers. Wedding or burial was to start, or just evensong.

I sat down in a chapel set aside for private prayer and opened Catharine as the third of her daughters, aged nearly four, came under suspicion. 'About three o'clock that afternoon,' Catharine said, 'Mr Page came in to see little Frances, and said he wished to call in fresh advice – not that he felt anxious about her, but that after the death of the other two it would be a greater satisfaction to have some one to watch her case with him. He wished for Dr Christison from Edinburgh, and we telegraphed for him, but found that he could not reach Carlisle till twelve next day.'

The awaited deeply muted opening sustained note from the organ moved out, almost beneath notice, into the spaces of the church. Off page my eye saw one or two people at intervals making for the chancel. The women had hats on. 'We then sent over to Brampton for Dr Graham, who came that evening and saw the little girl,' said Catharine. 'He did not think her very ill, and quite agreed in all that was being done for her. She lay oppressed with illness all that day, and was most good and sweet. She would rouse herself at once to take either food or medicine when desired, and when she had taken as much as she could would say, "No more, thank you, darling Mamma." She had a restless night, and when morning came she said, as on each other morning, "Now, Peachie, it is morning; I should like to say my prayer." We had a more comfortable account of her that morning, and when Dr Christison came he said she had a sharp attack of scarlet fever, but he quite thought the child would do well; he approved of all that was being done. The opinion of Dr Davy, who saw her that day, was the same. We went over to the other children, to cheer them through the window by this account. They were in good spirits, and we all hoped that a few more days would see our darling out of all danger. The Dean's brothers in Edinburgh were anxiously waiting for Dr Christison's report. He gave much more hope than fear to them. "But", he added, "it is a treacherous disease – none more so."'

My ears were lost in her language. An introit had gone unheard. But now a microphone hawked. Dearly beloved brethren, it said, the Scripture moveth us in sundry places to acknowledge and confess our manifold sins and wickedness; and evensong was now moving into its soothing rhythm of remission, protection against all perils and dangers of this night, and music in the minor: that the rest of our life hereafter may be pure and holy, so that at the last we may come to his eternal joy; and Catharine said, 'About ten o'clock, when the doctors came in, she was quiet, and they did not seem uneasy about her. Her Father and I were keeping watch with Jane till one, when Mrs Peach would take our place. Soon after the doctors left she became highly delirious, and so restless we could not keep her in bed; this lasted for some hours, and we became so much alarmed that when Mrs Peach came, we determined again to send for Mr Page. He came, and had her put in a hot bath. She was so weak that I thought she would sink under it, but when taken out she seemed better, and went into a sweet sleep. We also left her, and much exhausted went to bed. Tuesday she was ill, very ill, highly delirious, and worn out with fatigue. About four I had been out for a little drive, and went to look at my other darlings; they had been with our kind friend Mrs Dixon to the gardens at Knells, and had brought back some beautiful flowers. My Catty said, "Oh, Mamma, we have brought them for you." I said, "Keep them for me, darling, I could not bear them now; please God we are a little happier at Easter, I shall so like them." But when Easter came it brought no flowers to us.'

I set down the book on the pew. The strains of the Magnificat were bursting the eardrums of the vault. I longed to rush out and fall face to the sky on a patch of my own grass. But I was entoiled here until I had forced my way, within a growing bondage, to the end of the story. I had to know the outcome – but of what? Even this evensong would end in a query; all things did. 'I went in and stayed a few moments with my little Frances,' said Catharine; 'she was asleep and quietly so. I knelt down beside her; her life was in the balance, but Who was directing it? Should I take the choice upon myself, and crave at any cost the life of this sweet child now so very precious to us? I thought of their Home in Heaven to which Chatty and Susan were gone, and then the thoughts of the very brightest home I might hope to secure for this little lamb on earth. If her Home in Heaven was ready, should I wish to keep her here? No! I knelt and asked Him who could see all that was before her and us, to do as He saw fit with this our blessed child, and I knew that He would strengthen us.'

My mind strayed to the anthem, the organ elaborating an introduction to the poised voices of the choir. In the war as a boy I had wanted to discover any other organs in hiding, if they existed, somewhere out in the Hampshire countryside; the one in our parish church satisfied every desire except my appetite for more. These unknown instruments lay beyond the woods where enemy airmen had parachuted into the arms of soldiers – or local girls, some said. They were to be found deep in villages whose edges now and then caught a stray bomb. I stared at places on the map, a blob denoting a spire, a square a tower, a hinterland of adventure I had never penetrated. If I could find an instrument isolated enough I might dare to play it in my own hearing, just to see what I sounded like in that tongue of tongues.

At the weekend I cycled off. Hopes of a good organ were tinged with dread of a bad encounter. The hedges twittered threat. Larks trembled in the upper air of a dense afternoon. Nobody was about, yet the rural snooze seemed peopled by the invisible. My bicycle freewheeled as insects whirred about my head. I reached the first church, darkened within the antiquity of yews as impenetrable as history. Behind pines loomed a huge house, only an upper window clearing the trees. The church door echoed open on a vista sombrely narrowing through nave and aisle to a far altar. A shiver of cool enclosed me.

I averted my eyes from the altar and nipped at an angle between pews and stalls: a short cut to the organ. It stood in the gloom of an unlit transept. Whoever thought a source of music had to be hidden to be heard? My hand went out to open it up to inspection.

But the organ was locked. A pair of glass shutters cut off the console. Parades of stops were not quite legible behind the narrow panes. The manuals were untouchable. The stool was dully polished by a century of trousers better qualified than mine. Further afield must exist the bigger and better organs, open to view, off the map, more private. I had not gone far enough. The language was beyond me.

I came out into the hot remainder of the afternoon. That superior silence remained inside. I felt suddenly drained by the prospect of distance, thighs straining over the pedals, hands tightly sweating on rubber, the distance between this alien nature and the homely house where I was living. I had to learn how to play, then all doors would open for me.

You could not, averred the sub-organist when I next

saw him, be taught the organ. You had to learn the piano first. But where? He muttered that he had access to plenty of pianos that nobody knew about. I could practise next door; he would have a quiet word with the bank clerk who lived there. Time passed with difficulty. At home I awaited news of the hour and whereabouts of the first piano lesson that would lead to a mastery of the organ. A fortnight laboured past with nothing more dramatic than a bomb one night on the sawmills which splintered up piles of planks.

A week later after evensong the sub-organist handed me without a word a folded slip of paper. It was lined, at first glance resembling an underhand note in class. In front of other boys I furtively slipped it into my pocket. On the way home in the blackout I read it by shielded torchlight. The scribble was an assignation: it stated the hour for my first music lesson. The place was a school hall next to the bombed timber yard, which seemed both risky and right. A full moon flooded out between hasty clouds. Switching off the torch, I tingled with apprehensive pleasure.

On the appointed evening, the shadows long, I walked across the playground of a primary school I never knew existed. Nobody had yet cleared up the sawmills after the bomb. The hopscotch of the tarmac was littered with fragments of the raw material of wardrobes and bedroom floors never to be carpentered. The reek of resin polished the air. Wedged open with a parish magazine stood a door leading to a corridor that smelt of fear and infant sick. Classrooms gaped. Emptiness gave the school the air of a secret headquarters.

From afar, but as if within the head, came a blurred

murmur of chords in slow progression. In a large bare hall, at the foot of steps leading up to a stage, the sub-organist sat hunched at a piano, repeating ever more slowly that same series of chords, an ear cocked to catch their fall dying into the hall's gloom.

Two chairs were drawn up to the piano. He shifted his aside. He told me to sit down and play. A sheet of simple lullaby in an easy key confronted me. He said those little numbers were fingering. He told me I had five fingers on each hand. He instructed me to work it out for myself.

I doubted if I could.

He observed that if I didn't try I would learn nothing from him. He advised me to think of singing it. Then to play it.

A surge of fright like heat engulfed me. The notes were as large as targets, there to be picked off. My hands reached out to trigger the keys and I knew I could do it. The tune sang in my head. I heard a simultaneous lower voice, that of someone unseen, render the lower line. By a miracle my hands were working together, missing a note, hitting a wrong one, correcting, one falling behind the other, catching up too fast.

The sub-organist said nothing. When the last but one pair of notes joined in unison, my eye refocused the target at the top of the page and aimed at fewer misses a second time round. My feet were sweating in the cold, drops dripped down from my armpits and tickled my sides. My teeth lightly bit the tongue sticking half out of my mouth. I felt the man's slack intensity. Was it approval, had I done well? My aim wobbled, there was a clash. Then the one note again, played by both hands an octave apart, the end.

Not bad, said the sub-organist, and told me to learn it properly by next week.

Was that all? All that needed saying about a new language? All he could teach?

Not quite. For a spatulate finger touched my shoulder and, hands in pockets, the man stepped on to the stage. Here he looked ambiguously down at me as though about to pay me tribute in a speech or more likely expose my faults to an audience. He stood swaying as tall as an owl on the boards, glasses emitting a dull gleam of yearning. In the pause no command was barked or guidance given. I knew just what I was supposed to do. I felt pulled to do it. Yet I delayed. I wanted to be ordered, then praised.

The man jerked his head slightly, mouth opening with an odd salivary slap of tongue on palate. I walked up the steps, precipitating a flurry of activity on his part: bounding in lengthened stride from one side of the stage to the other, with wild sweeps of his arms, he drew the curtains, darkening the stage, then lumbered towards me. He placed his hands at intervals on my spine as if trying out a keyboard and, as before, pressed his tumescence against the vertical of my belly.

And at once this boy became a boy again, not a child learning the piano or a future organist or the acclaimed leader of a worldwide resurgence of interest in pipe-organs that would bring peace and pleasure to every nation on earth, in particular the filthy Huns for starting the war and the feeble French for giving in like they did; a boy not kicking out, not killing the enemy, putting up no resistance, not sniping from behind curtains in schools or hurling grenades from the top of church towers into the midst of a victory parade; but a boy falling into the enemy arms, being pillaged by the enemy, raped by the common soldier, rubbed up against war. The penis was between my upper thighs and I was shuddering with its efforts. The drawn curtains trembled as if someone were behind them. All of a sudden they might open to an audience of infants clapping and screeching at the spectacle of this imitation of a primitive pump engine demonstrated by a man and boy with their trousers down. A rush of heat blushed on my inner legs: a physics lesson, a howitzer retracting every time it fired, a machine-gun pumping lead into the infants who fell over and died with laughter stricken on their faces. The metronome was ticking at top speed between the muscles I used to run races, meanwhile on my shoulders his hands executed with perfect fingering an organ prelude by Bach.

These were not flashes of thought I was used to. They did not come and go in sequence. They were disordered on the edges of my brain by a lack of interest in the breathy aggression of this event, which made my body shake like the blast from the bomb on the sawmills. All I really saw was an empty stage on which I was cavorting against my will. No, against my desire. No, I had no desire. I had only myself. It was myself that was being attacked.

This time, with an effort that resembled a soldier half falling back to die, the sub-organist shot the wet seed all down the back of my legs where it lingered and dripped, hot and then cold, until a sluggishly produced hankie mopped it up. My socks were impregnated. The backs of my knees were going to have babies. The floorboards would soon be reproducing their kind.

Trousers were hoisted up. Curtains were drawn

back. There was no applause when the dying daylight revealed a space void of audience. Beyond the school windows the town was settling into a night that might again be disturbed by a scatter of bombs intended for elsewhere but hitting home.

Darkness was falling here in Carlisle too.

I had sat through evensong hardly hearing it and now the organ had rounded off a lengthy voluntary with a long echo and the vergers in a whisper were ushering out the last of the congregation. A few words of resonant gossip were exchanged at the south door. Unseen hands holding a glint of brass snuffed out candles in the chancel. Robed figures whitely withdrew and returned into a darkness only a touch blacker than their cassocks. This small world was emptying out into a larger one. On air scented with coal smoke I heard the choristers shouting freedom.

Three

I was reading in bed that night.

'Mrs Peach brought me my breakfast, which I tried to eat, and said, "Ah! we know now what it is to eat our bread in heaviness and sorrow of heart." I then said, "Have you heard yet of the other children?" She said, "I have not had the heart to ask." Soon after the Dean came in and Mr Page – oh, with what tidings! – Catty was ill . . .

'Mr Page came again soon to see dear Catty; she had been very sick; and he found her pulse so much reduced as to cause immediate alarm. He gave her champagne and water, which revived her, and she soon seemed in a more natural state . . . When her Father came in she seemed delighted to see him, and asked at once how Frances was. Miss Godding answered so as to evade an answer, and following him out of the room said she felt sure that to tell her would be fatal. He went back and prayed with his darling, and then returned to me. I had been meantime to see the form of my little Frances, as it lay in my room, with a look of unclouded innocence and beauty. I dared not stay too long, as what I craved for now was calmness of spirit to enable me to take my watch beside my first-born – that child who had called forth within us all that can be called forth of heavenly love and happiness – that child who had fulfilled our every wish, and who helped us with the others, and did her works in a way wonderful to contemplate. She and May grew together in the most undivided and beautiful way; must they also be separated? Who can tell the agony of our spirits? By the form of our little child we knelt, and sought for calmness and strength, whilst we earnestly sought that the life of our Catty might be granted to our prayers. I then went over, and with calmness, as if I had never been absent from her, took my place beside her. She was very glad to see me, threw her sweet arms round my neck, and asked me to pray with her, which I did. Her hair was all loose about her, that beautiful hair. I knew it must come off, and said, "My Catty, is not your hair very hot? shall I cut it off?" She calmly said, "Oh yes," and turned first to one side and then to the other while I cut it off, feeling all the time as if by this act I was giving up my child. I kept a little hair in water and burned the rest . . .

'About two o'clock in the afternoon of Good Friday she sank to sleep, and I left her with Miss Godding and the nurse and went over to the Deanery and put on my robes of deep mourning for the first time, not only now for Chatty and Susan, but for Frances also, and to follow her to her little grave. I could not bear to see another carried out and wait in agony at home. No, I felt that by going I might gain a little strength, and that it would comfort us to be together to give to the keeping of our Saviour the little one he had loved so well, and who now must sleep with her Chatty and Susan till He clothes their mortal bodies with the full beauty of immortality. We feared any sound for our Catty that would tell her what we were again going through, so we would allow no bell to toll, no carriages to come to the door. The great gate of the Abbey was kept closed as at night, and when three o'clock came, we crept out as quietly as possible from the Deanery with our little funeral.

'Sweet Catty, did an angel tell you that your Frances also was among the blessed redeemed whom you ever loved to think of and sing about? We had not dared to tell you, but I believe that God Himself had revealed to you the tidings of joy. She slept, but as the coffin that contained the form of her beloved Frances crossed the threshold of our door, she raised herself in her bed, and with a loud voice said, "Jesus cried, Lazarus, come forth. And he that was dead came forth, bound hand and foot with grave-clothes; and Jesus said, Loose him, and let him go." When she had said this, she lay quite still in a deep sleep. Sadly and solemnly did we meantime follow the lifeless form, and with the same blessed words of comfort and hope laid her in the very grave containing her Chatty and Susan, and then returned to church to give thanks to God for my own deliverance and the birth of my little Lucy. This was indeed a time of sad contrast to any before . . .

'We returned home in sad anguish of heart, and walked together about our garden. I said to my husband, "Oh, surely God is not going to take from us all our children!" He said, "Oh no; I feel almost sure God will spare us the rest: He will give us back our dear Catty. When Easter dawns, I believe and trust that hope will come back, and we shall see her really better." We could not contemplate the possibility of our Catty being taken. She was sleeping quietly, and I went to my room to nurse my dear babe.

'Easter Monday dawned, and we awoke, longing that it might bring us hope. Her Father went over at once to the other house. The doctors were there; he returned to me. I saw at once how it was. He said, "Catty is no better, and her throat has begun to swell." All my strength left me; I felt as if I could not live without her; and the agony I felt for his suffering was harder to bear than anything else. God was with us to strengthen us even in that darkness . . . She knew what we were suffering; no words were needed to communicate between her mind and ours. She could ever read at once in our face what was passing within. She had long seemed to us the connecting link that had kept us all together, in as sweet a bond of love as is ever given to a family on earth . . .

'Her Father said, "O my Catty, we do so love you, you have been such a treasure to us – everybody loves you, my child!" A look and sense of love more than any earthly love could give her burst on her dear soul, now nearly ripe for heaven; she turned and looked with a look we never can forget, at us, and then upwards towards heaven, and pointed there distinctly with her finger. While looking she seemed to see it open before her, and its light rested upon her enough even for our dull senses to perceive in part. While pointing upward I said, "She sees in heaven her Chatty, her Susan and Frances." When I mentioned the name of the latter, of whom before we had not spoken to her as taken from us, a brighter light came upon her, and again she pointed clearly and distinctly, and then with an earnestness no words can convey, stretched forth both her hands to be taken also, as if she saw, as most surely she did see, the angels waiting to convey her also to that place in the many mansions of our Father's house – into which three of her darlings had entered. I looked at Mrs

Peach and said, "She wants to leave us; she also wants to be taken home!" Her Father burst into floods of tears; she beckoned him to her, and stretching forth her dear hand she wiped the tears away, which she could never bear to see on his face, and tried in every way to comfort him. While she felt the gain to herself she did seem to feel for us . . .

'At length the agony was too much for me: my strength gave way; I could not stay beside her; I could not stay downstairs. Miss Godding took me over to the Deanery, and laid me on the bed and lay down beside me. I suppose I must have slept, for as the clock struck four I sat up in bed, and in a very agony of prayer seemed to follow the soul of my child through its parting conflict. I then prayed for those who had strength given them to be with her to the last. After that I again became unconscious till her Father came in to tell me it was all over. "Yes," I said, "she went at four." It was so – at four on Easter Tuesday, her baptismal morn, steadfast in faith, joyful through hope, and rooted in charity, she had so passed through the waves of this troublesome world that she had come to the land of everlasting life. That day ten years I had stood with her in my arms at the font, and given her into her Father's arms, who had baptised her in the name of the Father, Son, and Holy Ghost, who had signed her with the sign of the cross, in token that she should never be ashamed to confess the faith of Christ crucified, and to continue His faithful soldier and servant to her life's end. Yes, with earnestness of joyful love we laid our new-found treasure at our Saviour's feet that day, unflinchingly seeking that she might be His, and now with the fullness of sorrowing love we had laid her at

His feet for ever. My dear Mother, who stood by us rejoicing on Easter Tuesday 1846, no doubt welcomed her with joy unspeakable on Easter Tuesday 1856. Now she was gone home; she is blessed for ever. A few days before her illness began, she said to Miss Godding, "Oh, I do hope I may go to Church on my baptism day!" Blessed child, your wish was granted you indeed.

'At about six o'clock Miss Godding went, at my wish, to send my Husband. She found him still in that sad house. I threw my arms round him, and said, "Can you submit?" Yes, he could even do this, and he could strengthen me. How could I have borne all without his help and his prayers? We saw her once more together about four o'clock on the afternoon of Easter Tuesday. She lay with a wreath of white flowers round her dear head, and a sweet, quiet, thoughtful look on her face – she seemed to me so like her beloved Father; we knelt beside her and prayed as best we could. The next day no bell tolled, no carriages came to the door; the Abbey gate was kept locked; no sound was allowed to reach our darling May, and we stole out again to bear to its last resting-place the body of this beloved one.'

I turned out the bedside light.

Four

Nothing in my present life could, or did, interrupt that passage from Catharine on her first-born. I lay in bed, longing to give her solace. My mind ran beneath her words. She too lay in bed, sleepless for a while, then moving in and out of dreams.

Yet dreams had to exist in a somewhere of sorts. They were too much more real than apparent reality to vanish without trace. Catharine had nurtured in me an inability to believe that all human experience went the way of all flesh. Yet over the century since you were alive to the full, Catharine, I had grown up enough to have no need of faith in a personal eternity. So what happened to the art which night after night we all produced, when utterly alone or half in the arms of someone: dreams that made dark sense of all the things that struck us as senseless about daylight – what of all that?

Each morning I bought the paper in Kennington or fetched bread from our town in Wales. I exchanged a few words with others who had just got up. How warmly the moment of meeting might be affected, perhaps was, by the tacit understanding that the night we had all just shared had been spent slipping into permanent form whatever antics our brains had performed during the night when detached from the disappointments of being conscious. But we kept our silence. The archive could not tolerate recognition of its existence, any more than the invisible man wanted to lose his advantage over the ruck of humanity, any more than God could exist at all if he were definable, any more than Walter wanted his secret life to be exposed save on his own terms.

The archive was trying to shut me up, without encouraging me to stop believing in it. It simply wanted no publicity. Dreams had their own way of mutely defeating attacks on their integrity. Nobody knew for sure: dreams still seemed to us godlike – they were like God; we worshipped them without thinking, we felt them at dawn forever sliding away from us while we longed to catch them, we suspected we needed their humour as they slipped out of our grasp, and we woke up exasperated, crossly missing life passing us by. Now we could only plod through the day's aimless reaches: which were, unknown to us, to be converted by night into masterpieces which once more by morning we would forget.

And then again bread, milk, the paper, a raised hand in Kennington, a greeting in Wales, a worldwide conspiracy of silence. Dreams did not really exist (we all colluded in assuming) any more than faith did.

Five

Again I had to go west to Wales to dispose of the house.

On the train I saw herons musing on water close to the tracks that led nowhere. Wilderness backed off into mountains that had no end. The farmers next door were having a problem raising the money. They were busy in private trying to sell on our house with a view to keeping the land: a mess of local deals that were breaking up my past and dismantling our children. I also had to keep on the move the other past I was exploring to find out whether it had a future. So along with me in the compartment sat Walter, peeling back the petticoats as his express whizzed through Woking, and Catharine travelling south to the diocese of London after committing her pain to paper at the as yet unlocated Hallsteads.

It was God's gift, sex, like death. It brought man and woman together in a sacred act, as often as possible, with intent to populate the globe with men and women more to God's liking than hitherto. God approved of progress, so our system of reproduction was designed as a ceaselessly vigilant corrective to its earlier mistakes. Bed was moral.

In Hampshire in the war I met my first girl only because I was billeted with her parents. We were thrown together in a red-brick semi too small to be shy in; the few rooms cramped you into contact. Opposite lay a soggy paddock where she proudly kept her ponies. She was always teasing me to come out riding. To convert her to my own enthusiasm I picked from the map an organ in a hamlet some miles out of town. I was to show off an unexplored territory, then conquer it. Without knowing why, I wanted her to be impressed.

The horse she led me to was small, chest height. I threw myself on and wobbled in the saddle. The pony shook under me as if consumed by laughter. The girl snorted behind, steam pluming from her steed's black nostrils. I rode down Vicarage Hill plunging to my death. I bounced past Tanhouse Lane speechless. Vaguely I heard her clip-clopping at my side as a motor car roared past me.

From on high I stared down at the outskirts of town, persons on foot who at our approach slewed away in fear. The girl dismounted to open gates, jodhpurs tightening as she bent. Fields enclosed us. I peered at the secrecy of the woods ahead. Beneath me the pony eased its joints into a territory that suited it, the lure of water meadows. Before us lay the simple cross on the map that stood for the church.

The church turned out to be more of a chapel. It stood isolated in aristocratic parkland. Deer roamed within walls topped by jagged glass. Order and authority glittered in every window of the distant mansion. The scene hinted at the sublime. But in the shadows of trees a few untended khaki lorries were lined up. They bore the markings of a Canadian regiment based near a village I knew whose location was nonetheless a strict secret. Petrol hovered in the air.

The ponies sniffed and whinnied as if sensing danger. Hers was mettlesome, mine affrighted. Hers dashed suddenly ahead. Mine was stuck trembling beneath a tree, champing on a low branch, eyes wide. As soon as I caught her up, panting hard from an uncontrolled canter that only just let me hang on, the two ponies nuzzled each other's blackly sweating heads, and her eye met mine.

We were at the chapel.

I felt I must make some statement (yet I was too puffed), speak some words about the uniqueness of organs (but I could think of none), end with a profession of faith in their power (which was beyond describing). The girl held her reins tightly, lips pursed. I tried for a syllable or two. Nothing emerged. Someone must be listening out there, even for a whisper. A sniper was concealed in the yew. An unseen force was advancing on the mansion to destroy it in seconds. There was not much time. I slid off the pony, attaching the reins to a bald twig of the evergreen. Unsteady but aware of a swagger, I marched to the porch and said over my shoulder, 'Let's see what's inside.'

The main door was locked. I stared at the cast-iron handle and wrenched again. Again it clattered and did not give. Her impatience loomed somewhere above me. Her pony snickered. The afternoon hummed with silence. Out there the opposing forces must be nearing each other, as yet undetected. Tension mounted, sweat broke out on my body, the assault closed in.

Still on horseback, the girl ambled towards a small high window at the side of the chapel. No doubt it gave on to a vestry. It was of plain leaded glass with a catch inside. She reached out, rattled it; the frame shifted. With a poised crop she gave the window a neat tap. A diamond of glass fell inwards and clinked on stone. Up in her stirrups, she thrust her crop inside to release the catch, flicked the window open. Her pony backed a couple of paces. She waited smugly.

A low brick offered a foothold. I grazed my hands clambering up the wall. I bruised an elbow squeezing through. As I jumped inside not quite head first in a tumble of limbs, I tore a knee on a brass candlestick, blood seeped. Sitting dazed on a tombstone of black marble I breathed in, while gazing at antiquated commandments inscribed in a frieze round the walls, the print dim.

This vestry door had a key on the inside. I let the girl in. A few moments later I was sitting next to her on the organ stool. Something seemed wrong somewhere. This was quite a pretty instrument with a frontage of decorative pipes. But they were fake. I blinked. I had brought her not to the organ of my dreams, but to a harmonium.

Pumping it with my feet, I played my impromptu with due contempt. Mechanically the instrument wheezed out the all too familiar notes. It was a misery of a machine, an assembly of thin reeds that set the teeth on edge. There was not a whisper of declamatory power, no trace of syrupy undertone. Yet the girl looked almost starry with wonder, her glance passing slowly from the dull keyboard to my face as if to share a prime pleasure: as though I mattered more than the instrument and strangely I did not want that.

At this moment the vestry clattered as a brass candlestick hit stone. Drawing in her breath hard, the girl pushed her hand against mine on the stool. Into the chapel on tiptoe stepped a soldier. He failed to take off his tin hat in church. With quiet purpose he moved down the aisle towards us. He raised the hand not holding the stengun, put a warning finger to lips smudged with charcoal. Behind him ranged another soldier in the same bent posture, gun barrel raking the empty pews. Others followed at intervals of five yards, all ignoring the pair of us on the stool, carrying out a silent attack on an area suspected of containing an enemy. At the main door, without trying it from the inside, the corporal turned, with a sweep of his arm ordering retreat. Slightly speeding up the slow motion, yet with no more noise, the group backed out through the vestry, to exit by the very door the girl had earlier waited for me to open.

We looked at each other wide-eyed. Were we seeing things? Around us the chapel was as unchanged as ever. An unaccountable urge pulled at my stomach muscles. She slapped a hand quickly to her mouth. At the same moment we began shaking. The laughter first shook in silence, but then control lapsed, a high giggle escaped, echoed, and within seconds we were writhing on the stool, not touching, arms wrapped tightly round our bodies for containment, eyes brimming.

Close outside a burst of firing jolted us to our senses. Again fear filled the tiny church. Her hand went out to me. A harsh voice from a direction hard to ascertain was giving commands even harder to hear. We were surrounded by invisible men whose purposes I could not fathom.

In the end the fuss died down. The armies retreated. 'Phew,' said the girl, slowly raising her eyes to me. In their blue I saw a stir that was beyond relief. We had a lucky escape, but the tension still held her. On the stool the round of her knee touched mine. Only a quarter-inch of clothes and a foot or two of quiet air separated our bodies, which seemed both to draw closer and to be trapped in a spell. Catching my breath, I lost all power of speech. With an irrational surprise I felt the brains draining from my head and dropping vertiginously to the swell lower down. Her lips moved slightly apart as if about to speak, but instead they darted forward, flickered on my cheek, found my mouth, latched on, and opened wide to let her tongue in, and in seconds I was both suffocating under the impact and raging with desire so intense as to have been hitherto beyond imagining. Still seated aslant the organ stool, me with legs under the keyboard, hers facing the church, she thrust her tongue with a pumping rhythm between my teeth and halfway to the larynx as, headily short of oxygen, I felt incapable of realising that her hand had descended to my area of commotion as though trying to calm it down. Her fingers patted it inside the school trousers. Her palm stroked it. It was all too much. The event I had been awaiting unwittingly for fourteen years, as blinding as the arrival of a faith, occurred – on and on, but far too fast. Before I had time even to glance into a future transmogrified by the love between man and woman, she irritably brushed down her jodhpurs, retracted her mouth, stared briefly at the map of an equatorial country imprinting itself on my flannels, winked, slipped off the stool and was away.

A moment later I was lifting her clumsily but with a possessive blush in my chest towards the vestry door I had unlocked. Her curves fitted my arms. The ponies stood in the hushed park unharmed. A vicious stab of interest in the war caught me as I glimpsed her leg tense and swing over the saddle. I sniffed cordite on the air.

We rode home chastened, shaken, harmoniums forgotten, to find hubbub in the house. First news had come through of an invasion of the Continent. The wireless in the kitchen crackled like fire. I was grown up. She was thirteen.

Back in the Welsh night, exhausted from clearing out the house that was almost sold, measuring the value of possessions long ignored, piling books even longer unwanted for tomorrow's visit from the local knacker, I dreamed in great peace. I awoke just once, again knowing that we were all just factories, daily stocking up on the raw material that was processed by night into other forms, then fixed in a dimension beyond the reach of conscious search. They passed outside time without hindrance. They eluded memory on purpose. The thought dispelled, with final humour, the notion that I was meant to recount to others such remnants of narrative hotchpotch as I recalled in tatters. I need bore breakfast no more. All my best work had slipped into the archive at dead of night.

Six

Back in London I crossed the Thames at lunchtime to an organ recital at a City church. I wanted the triumphal sound of that instrument to stir both me and memory: it was an old passion. At home I popped into my pocket a paperback of *The Invisible Man*, so of course I walked over Southwark Bridge with a sense of being followed: nobody ever grew up. The recital was meant for office workers in their lunch break. Free coffee and biscuits tempted the faithful and bribed the unbelieving: we were still all children.

I had earmarked a Fleet Street wine bar for lunch afterwards, alone with my book. Meanwhile on Ludgate Hill, rising towards St Paul's, I kept looking over my shoulder. The chilling malevolence of the invisible man had scared me in childhood and now his latterday equivalent, still unidentified, was scaring the child in me. An opulent car going west swished to a sharp halt at a crossing, narrowly missing two secretaries with a sneer of brakes. Apologies were hard to distinguish from abuse.

The church within was rinsed of the divine by popular disuse. Any lambs and angels in the stained glass had been shattered in the blitz. Now the glass was plain. A sentimental token of a Christ in plaster crucified the wall behind the altar. I fingered the book, not quite liking to read out of respect for the organist, now digitally limbering up in the loft. Not for the first time I saw that music lovers had a look that pined for something the other side of music.

I sat back in my pew and stared around at the lack of the numinous. The invisible man had, Wells said, 'elaborate plans for the complete realisation of the advantages my invisibility gave me over my fellowmen'. I could never remember his name but now saw between my fingers that it was Griffin. I thought of the grips of his very strong hands, his habit of tripping people up, his treatment of life as a practical joke devoid of humour. I saw him, or rather failed to see him, on the screen of my boyhood in Chichester when I believed in him as much as in the huge dark organ.

The film's images whirred back to mind with their original force. A monstrous figure loomed out of a blizzard to descend in rage on a village in Sussex within reach of my organ expeditions. He wore a clown's nose and unlikely side-whiskers. To ingest eggs and bacon he was forced by the camera to show that he had no face. A fork floated in the air to the sound of spectral mastication. In due course his clothes scattered in panic all over the shop and nobody was there at all: only this hard dry voice insinuating threat in the empty air.

The rebuilt Wren church creaked and hushed. The invisible man was wholly immoral – hurting people, firing houses, stealing money, prompting his own father's suicide, not unlike, on the whole, most gods, if not God. His violence lay seething in the book in my pocket. Behind my eyes he still haunted the film I saw that afternoon on the edge of war.

First on the programme was a Bach prelude and fugue. I closed my eyes. Music, as usual, was hypnogogic in

168

setting off images in the half-dark of being almost asleep. In Hampshire I had populated my environment with items taught in school, taught as gospel. The hills round Alton were secret repositories of the classical. The Minotaur was fuming in Ackender Woods. The Wey at its source opposite our semi was the Tiber on its flow to Rome. I had Xenophon marching across Flood Meadows in an unparsable surge towards victory, while at the pharmacist in the High Street my mind tricked Oedipus into being eye-tested for new and useless glasses. There seemed no point in not bringing legends back to life; back into life.

Our town had plenty of stables on the outskirts. The divine birth could have taken place in any of them, but I picked the ample stabling of the vicarage, up the ladder into the hayloft of which I was once a fortnight led by the sub-organist to await, if not for long, his pleasure. I had found it as familiar as a crib. Cuts of sun shot between the ill-fitting planks of the walls. In dusty haloes light blobbed the floorboards from missing tiles in the roof. A hay-filled manger in the stable below had only yesterday been vacated by a baby who was going to alter my life two thousand years later. One or two of the three wise men were drinking a farewell glass of port with the vicar, while the shepherds had gone back to their flocks on the slopes that lifted from the Basing-stoke Road. The cast of the virgin birth had dispersed, while this male member yet again aped the act of thieving my virginity. Meantime in church, somewhat aged by now, balding and bent, Jesus was wheezing up the steps of the pulpit at the parish church in the guise of the Revd W. G. M. Hutchison, MA, shortly to die on the cross of heavy smoking.

At the organ the same tune as before entered higher up the scale in pursuit of the fugue. I thought of the invisible man emerging from concealment to hang just over my shoulder, his breath at my ear, scorning whatever I was reading, even *The Invisible Man*, longing to wolf the ham I would soon be eating in the wine bar, half starved and crying out for vengeance. What was it, what, who was he? It was as if something lodged awkwardly within me had escaped, and run amok in the anarchy of the outer world.

More of the organ's voices entered at other levels persisting in the melody that twisted in and out of the statement that had opened it. The church was packed tight with sound. My attention flickered away from the abundance of noise. In the loft I glimpsed Walter seated at the organ. His hands were stretched to the keyboards. Between his busy arms, squatting frontally on his lap, her white thighs gartered above the knee clasped round his besuited back, a naked woman was moving slowly up and down on him. Her expression was ecstatic, her eyes rolling to the music, her arms almost garotting him. It was Catharine. Walter's trousers were halfway to his ankles as he struggled manfully with the pedal part. His ears were awash with a grand progress that arrived after many a complexity at the triumph of a solution. He finished.

As the strains of the organ echoed off, a spasm of applause came, and faded. Elgar's organ sonata was the next to break the silence, putting me in mind of a boyhood when every sweep of downland contained a thicket which the invisible man had inhabited. He might still be there. For somewhere in those hills not far from my wartime Hampshire, according to Wells's story, his suitcase of knowledge had been stolen by a tramp. In revenge for being teased by a dancing non-shape that must have struck him as a god, a tramp had nicked his culture: the books wherein lay locked the secrets of Griffin's return to visibility. And, yes, he had hit the tramp. Griffin had knocked an inferior all over the green-muffled hangers – and, in good melodramatic style, paid the price. Never again could the invisible man rebecome himself – until, as he forecast, he died. Then he would fade back into sight. To a world which he had hoped by his absence to dominate, he would return in a second coming too late to be of any use.

In that space the Elgar sounded huge. I knew in an instant that what had been been haunting me for years, for much of my lifetime, was no outside force. More sinisterly it was an unknown in myself, a person who passed in and out of me as though I were his residence, someone who had got hold of my freehold and, by law or custom unassailable, lived impregnably within it.

A look at the plot of the book on my knee found this invisible man in department stores, a dint embedded in a mattress, or standing unseen in a pair of shoes, always on the verge of causing chaos. He was a curtain with nothing behind it, a wardrobe as void as space, a swelling display of lingerie without a buttock or a breast in sight; he lay on a sofa that looked as emptily comfortable as a philosophy. His habit of passing beyond human perception, as Wells put it, hypnotised me. It gave him the capacity to move outside time, for a spell to become timeless. It turned him into a dream.

Again my eyes closed. I thought of people next door in the Kennington Road or round in the square, of couples in bed in streets extending far beyond the local.

I viewed their comings and goings, glimpsed through a window, just missing them as they slipped round a corner, as more important than mine, even significant. They had caught on. I had not caught up. It was always the things I was not told, but had to guess, which lent these people a quality, a mystery, that never strayed into the obviousness of my own life. In Wales it was the screams of our small children eating into the night, inconsolable sounds that had to do with a life into which I kept not tuning. It sounded as if I were missing it all. Back gardens disturbed me for fear the neighbours were up there in bed proving me inadequate to their insights. I lacked their fluency in life. They were all seeking if not an explanation, at least an extension of the possibilities. But was I?

Here in London, working through the tomes on Tait's life, I had fallen more and more in tune with this addictive solitary, my hero. His urge to be prominent in the big bad world was endearingly virtuous. He had been well trained to train people younger than himself; his own upbringing fitted him to bring up others. He gave boys at Rugby the strict devotion he would apply to his daughters as one by one they were born into his affections. I too had taught. As their tutor in American universities the students had schooled me to think of them if not as offspring, then as aspects of myself. The key to teaching was warning them off my pitfalls. Children of my own had the effect of concentrating my whole class into one vulnerable student, dependent for the moment on my knowledge, but absorbing its benefits fast enough to gain the strength to reject it. Good education instructed you in what was best kicked aside, what better to hold on to.

I saw my two children, the girl eighteen, the boy fifteen, as much in terms of fear as of delight. Helpless as infants, they extorted every service at any moment. Contrary to assumption, they seemed more vulnerable as they grew older; years piled on risks. They were always in desperate need of things which we as parents did not recognise, though we longed to give everything within (or beyond) reason. The more they set about treading on the toes of their own lives, the less they wanted advice on how to walk. Risk to children had scarcely lessened since the middle of the last century; perils just differed. When three, our son glugged down half a bottle of cough linctus and, while we were phoning the doctor in panic, he climbed into our old Renault 5 steeply parked, and in an infantile master-piece of co-ordination released the handbrake and shot it out of gear. It rolled downwards gathering speed but slowly hit a wall. He emerged unharmed. The car was a write-off.

Death was good at keeping its methods up to date. There was little to choose between the Tait family wiped out by scarlet fever in the midst of Carlisle and the Jurgensen family crushed to death on a motorway outside Paris at seventy miles an hour. Human error had a near synonym: human ignorance. Each was equally at fault: in the early instance, failure of diagnosis, lack of cure, or delay in quarantine; in the modern case, failure of judgement, a car in a hurry, inadvertence.

When I looked in mirrors, eyes watering as I shaved, I stared at the prospect of losing either of our two, whom with self-mockery as frequent as irritation, we regarded as struck all too fatally in our own image; developments of ourselves; variations on a theme their

173

ears were still too young to pick up – but the future's preferred alternative to their parents.

At an extreme, may it never happen, my eyes looked at my dead daughter or the remains of my son over a reach of feeling that was as intolerable in concept as furthermost space: their bodies lying flat, hers squashed like a pigeon on the road, his flopped sideways off a mattress from excess of a drug, both so far outdistancing any experience of mine that I could not bear their having succumbed to it without my say-so or ever again accept accident as a reason, as an explanation, for any bloody thing at all in life or out of it.

At these moments in the mirror, I had no wish particularly to live any longer. I just wanted the children to outdo me. I needed them to get shot of my future which was consuming their present and shortly to be their past. I wished their pleasures to transcend mine. The taste of life in their nostrils, the reek of it in their blood, the insight of sound in their ears, the resonance of what their eyes caught, the blind touch that sprang open all their senses: that was the lot I wanted for them, in plenty, over years, for good.

Meanwhile, Almighty God, who hast poured upon us the new light of thine Incarnate Word, such was the power wielded by my having been present at their birth: to realise that they were the world, without my having to think the world of them. From the first these babies fought the present all-out, crying out for a future to supplant it. Their bath times were oceans unexplored. Their playrooms were world wars.

In the City church the Elgar sonata smoothed me awake by ending. Again the notion came to me – a dream just slipping away – that the terrifying strength of the invisible man lay in Griffin's being inside me, a thing of spitting violence and cruelty only just leashed, which my conscious allied to my conscience did their busy best to control, in an effort to prevent my noticing any conflict. And I thought of the griffin in all its shivery definitions: an imaginary animal with a lion's body and an eagle's beak and wings; a new-comer in the East, a novice; a pony never before entered for a race; a watchful guardian, especially over a young woman; a duenna: and all those descriptions seemed in that instant to be spine-chilling versions of me, and all wicked, the me I never cared to know, the one brushed under the carpet, the skeletal self in my own cupboard.

In the porch, music lovers drifted off to the reek of boiled coffee. Spell it out, I thought, spell it out: you are haunted only by yourself. The invisible man is within. At times he taunted you with a future, at others he agonised you with your past. He was telling me that what I possessed in, or of, the present was nothing. He added for good measure that illusion was itself illusory, unless I thought that any idea of God was but a shadow of the limitless opportunities which I had within me and was endlessly disappointing.

I trailed along to the wine bar off Fleet Street, ate some smoked salmon, drank some white burgundy, consumed some ham, swilled down some claret, and enjoyed the racket of others taking pleasure in this plod of unrepeatable moments which life casually was, and I reread at a skim from start to finish this halfway numinous novel about the man who had been invisibly inside me all the decades I had considered him either an implacable enemy waiting to pounce, or a sick figment of someone else's imagination, or God. By the time I rose to go home the present had gone back to work and a girl was sweeping up the sawdust around my feet.

Part V

One

But I still had to find Hallsteads and one spring morning I set out south from Carlisle. Against all the modern evidence – of maps, local records, hearsay – I knew the house lay somewhere, as much a fact as during Catharine's occupancy, if altered beyond retrieval. I needed to find whatever there was: a site or a sighting. For Catharine the house had proved a saviour which drew her out of hell, the sedative of lakeland lapping her in an astral silence. For me it might offer yet another chance to prove faith believable, or at worst round off her story.

In these weeks of readying our departure from Wales and steadying myself, a dread dogged me: if I failed to locate Hallsteads I would never make Catharine my own, yet never be able to forget her. The story would spin on. I would have effectively nowhere to live. A jealousy of the past sharpened this morning, as I looked for the roads the Taits had taken during their retreat from the void of the Deanery. And jealousy it was, jealousy of their intimacy heightened by grief, and of all things beyond attainment.

I had caught the habit from Geneviève. When her daughters had been dead ten years, she was haunted by the existence in Paris of the particular lovers they would never have, men even now eye to eye with girls other than hers at café tables, taking strangers in their arms. On an equally touched level I ached for Catharine as a sweetheart holding hands across the divide of a century, an object of desire now dust. Her very spirituality emitted a whiff of aphrodisiac. But most and best I saw her as a tenderly human guide to the manners – purity, prayer, propriety, sheer goodness – now lost in me, a language I could only stutter.

Turning off the motorway after Penrith, braking into the blind corners of the lanes towards Ullswater, I stopped in a layby of shadow for a pee. A burn tossed noisily over the rocks below, a breeze gurgled overhead in the birches. An authentic shiver went down my spine. Tait had paused or passed here; and of him too I felt envy. I zipped up. Back in the car I sat for a moment, their book on my lap, locked in a premonition of disappointment. As with faith, the prospect of not finding Hallsteads at all was unbearable enough to delay my looking for it. Tait's prose ran on in slow counterpoint to the sounds of stream and trees. It was his first mention of their loss.

'Then on a day in the early spring of 1856,' he said, 'the clouds darkened and a change came upon us with the suddenness and overpowering force of a thunderstorm. She must herself describe this change in her own words. Suffice it to say here that in six weeks we laid five loved daughters in the churchyard at Stanwix within sight of our old Cathedral, and near the quiet waters of the Eden. Many a prayer had been offered up in Carlisle and elsewhere for our afflicted family, but God saw it to be for our good to take our children to Himself. Early in April, the day of the funeral of the last who died, we fled with our newborn baby, and were followed by our dear little son, to take refuge for a few days among the hills at Moffat, almost afraid that we should not be received in any lodging from the alarm which the fever that visited the Deanery had caused. After a little time we moved to the country she loved so well on the banks of Windermere; there we rested a fortnight, and presented our baby to be received into the Church at Bowness. The summer found us, by the kindness of our friends the William Marshalls, slowly recovering from the shock which had uprooted us from the Deanery, in the pleasant house they lent to us on Ullswater; soothed between the months of May and September by wandering with our dear Craufurd amid the most lovely scenery, in perfect retirement, watching the ever-changing colour on the hills around us, as week followed week in the advance from spring to autumn. She returned with me to Carlisle for the opening of the restored Cathedral in June, when we stayed with our friends the George Dixons. We never slept in the Deanery again. The shock had been overpowering. But as in the quiet country home which had been lent to us, we cherished our dear little son and baby girl, and read together and prayed together, and bathed our spirits in the beauties that surrounded us, by God's mercy there came over us a holy calm.'

A holy calm. I drove on, the old map beside me: lake white as a sheet, mountains a thunderous black. An entire promontory was marked Hallsteads in italics that covered dozens of acres. By contrast the latest Ordnance Survey's superior detail identified in colour any number of properties on the shore, but not the house I sought. I steered along the wriggles of penmanship. Steep shadings of hillside rose above the car. The two maps, then and now, lay in crumpled contours over the rear seats, as much a couple of concertinas as a palimpsest, piling up at my back both geography and history, and music if not metaphor.

It was all too much, including the comparisons with Wales. These were in full view, too intricately touching to be easy to look at: sheep in blobs of notation syncopated on the green slopes, making a dotty accompaniment to the melody of the hills inscribed on blue sky.

What was it about Hallsteads? It was simply an unknown house I wanted to live in. In the wake of the sale of our Welsh place I was eager, on a plane distinct from any exchange of money or the greed of possession, to make an offer for it. I knew I would feel at ease there if only it existed. I had our bits of furniture – a nice decrepit Welsh dresser, a long desk to command a view of Ullswater – which required storage space. I had a whole life behind me that needed a home in front of me. All the children's old board games and dumb animals would fit into the attics. I saw myself with the help of stalwarts manoeuvring a four-poster into the best bedroom and maids plumping up feather mattresses. I put my ear to walls thick enough to betray no sexual activity next door. I tested the floors of corridors that would never creak when gentlemen on the roam tiptoed towards the wrong ladies. By far outnumbering the day's social saloons were these chambers of the night. They were apartments for the production of a host of dreams, in a house where all of us in this adventure were to live, contemporaneously, the Hallsteads I had seemed up to now to stand no chance of running to earth.

I had only a couple of lines to go on, from a topography of Cumberland published in 1860, four years after the girls died. The manorial rights belonged to William Marshall, Tait's host. The house was 'seen on the Skelley Neb promontory to the left – the grounds circling which are beautifully laid out'. With instant shame I knew that on the earlier search I had given up too soon, as if really wanting to find Hallsteads a ruin or a figment, preferring then to leave Catharine's haunt to the imagination: a shrine invisible.

A hundred yards beyond the point where months ago I had halted my fieldwork stood an elaborate Italianate structure now belonging to the Forte chain. Reception was baffled by my enquiry, so summoned the manager, who had lived twenty years hereabouts; the name Hallsteads meant nothing to him. But his files held an old plan of the place, which he kindly sloped off to find. The luxuriant kitsch of the hotel was a far-fetched attempt to spruce up for suburban tastes a country house ill suited to the austerity of the Taits. This was more like Walter's territory for those lulls when he treated his lust to a weekend out of town, as much to stalk classier game as to exploit the maids. I smelt bacon and coffee. The manager slid back from nowhere with a photocopy showing that the acres bordering this mansion had belonged to William Marshall. Such immense gratitude filled me that I almost ordered the full breakfast.

Next door the drive, wriggling through stands of pine rising high out of massed rhododendrons, led past a stableyard with tower and clock. All looked disused. The trees had outgrown their strength. On the up-to-date map the property was marked as the lakeland head-quarters of Outward Bound. The house proper had one long drab side of windows ending in a portico. In the grounds nobody was about. All was as mute as memory.

I entered to a swell of noise. Youth was all over the place. Talk hammered back and forth. Boys bagged up in tracksuits pushed up and down narrow passages, girls flocked round the flutters of pinned-up shorthand on the noticeboard, doors slammed. It was the start of the day, and the acoustics were strained to bursting. I felt old, but involved, but resigned, but happy, all in a rush. An instructor showed me, framed in the hall, the first intake of Outward Bound photographed against the portico in the 1950s. On the lintel above the force of their smiles was painted the one word I wanted to see: Hallsteads. I was home and dry.

With everyone's permission I wandered at will. The frontage on to the lake was narrow, scarcely grand. Low-slung bay windows bulged at the stupendous view. From a lawn more stubble than sward I picked out Catharine's window; I was guessing not assuming that she composed so private a record in her bedroom, the whereabouts of which I was divining not taking for granted. The smallish garden, confined by not much of a fence, no longer bore more than a trace of the laid-out grounds of yore; horticulture was evidently not on the curriculum here. A field containing a motionless bull sloped down to the shore of the glassy lake. It had the pathos of a photograph. Here Catharine took exercise at her wit's end, while Tait toiled back from Carlisle after a day's decanal effort. On a cairn opposite the portico a plaque recorded that in this place the young represented present, past and future as they adventured their way into life. Again in myself, on reading the words cut out of stone, I felt a surge of youth, idealism, tears, age. I was past all that, but as present as ever.

The old Hallsteads had become in effect a barracks,

the parlour a classroom, the dining room a mess. Built for subtlety of cohabitation between master and servant, the country house survived only in outline. For Walter any such mansion as Hallsteads had been a pander to satyriasis. Whoever tapped inopportunely on a door, behind which he verged on orgasm, was a spur to his gusto. Any risk raised his game. Among this mob of athletic girls awaiting today's assignment at Outward Bound, their curves muffled in clothing less provocative than protective, it was just as easy to imagine Archie making a conversion as Walter a killing. Here, stripped of its old trimmings of comfort, was the spot for that unlocated weekend (Walter pumped up illicit excitement by never naming dates or places) when he visited a sickly aunt, only to find his cousin Hannah nursing her with the help of the maid called Bates, cue for hanky-panky in earnest.

I had Walter's second volume locked up in the boot of the Saab, again booked for its annual service. In the remains of the garden I stood voyeuring the myopic windows that overlooked the view. 'The fog had thickened,' Walter said, 'the room was darkish, all was as silent as the grave . . . I thought not of who she was or who I was – my prick was stiff and throbbing. I pulled her to me and we kissed and kissed. "Oh, I can't breathe – leave off, Walt," said she in a soft voice. "Let me love – let us – who will know – let's do it," said I, pressing her thighs, slipping my hand towards her knee. "Oh, don't – oh, don't." A stoop, a lift, and my hand was on her naked thighs . . .'

It felt good: Dean Tait riding back to Hallsteads with his mind on his wife, reining in desire out of rectitude, longing for the dark to close on those light nights of the north, sitting at dinner perplexed by his pity for Catharine curdling his need of her; then, when all was quiet, pacing a few yards of passage to her side: all supposition, but Archie had long been aware of sex as the bodily force that pressed the urges of the spirit, an appetite that brooked as little inhibition as hunger or thirst: so now, alone at last, going the final lap to conceive a child which might die in infancy in the arms of Jesus, his want of fatherhood climaxing in the depths of the mother, driving a stream of seed unseen into the future of his century, making love to her despair and his own hope: here in the hills in the silence; making up for, making love for, the five girls who died in the space of little more than a menstrual period – girls born as heartily of faith as lustily of passion.

At Hallsteads, as I stood, yesterday's bedroom windows rattled to the cries of today's youth dying to churn their present into a future. Meanwhile in coition's melting aftermath the two Taits lay lightly in each other's arms at the outset of a dream, heads close, swooning into the unconscious of an Ullswater night of long ago: bodies, eased of lust, now easing out dreams into the unlocatable non-dimensional, inconceivable gumption of the archive – yes, the archive, its wisdom, a wisdom without parallel or precedent.

No one could venture an opinion about your dream. A dream had the advantage of being beyond sharing, so invited no comment. The climate in which a dream flared behind your eyes had a tendency to be graded by your whereabouts: how far from urban noise I was, how remote from being busy. Dreams had preferences without being pushy. They liked having access to plenty of country houses. They were often at home abroad. A change of temperature, indeed any fluctuation in weather, at once vivified a dream. Rain thudding down a window in Wales touched them off. Postprandial snoozes in hammocks in the Languedoc brought them out in a sweat. Uneasy nights in the tropics hotted up dreams by several degrees on the thermometer of nightmare. But all along I knew, every icy night or equatorial siesta, that I was being pushed over into the afterworld, the life free of time: for specific signs of which all religions sought in vain. I often dropped off by day in my upright chair in the hope of catching on the hop this evanescent eternity. But I never stopped reminding myself that I was spending eight hours a night, a third of my lifetime, constructing my own paradise out of the great indigestible mass of factors, raw elements, amorphous events, irrelevancies, which were crammed daily by my senses into my mind, where they lodged in blockage until I felt tired enough to give them a chance of freedom by lying down and closing my eyes.

Not only the dreaming but the writing too came from within yards of where I now stood at Hallsteads. To the last of the five daughters, nine-year-old May, her mother Catharine was saying, ' "You must rest now, perhaps you may be stronger another time, and then you shall tell us what to say." I then went to nurse baby. When I came back Miss Godding said, "She has had such a smile upon her face!" I went to her, and she smiled at me, but oh it was a smile fearful to witness, and fearful was the agony it gave me. About half-past five she said, "I am going to say my prayers," and closing her eyes she continued in prayer for some minutes, and then, in a whisper which we could plainly hear, she repeated the Creed. She then called her Father and said, "I have said my prayers and am going to sleep, will you say a little prayer with me?" We knelt down and prayed with her; she then called me to say a prayer with her, and said, "Good night, dear Mamma, I am going to sleep . . ."

'All was quiet, and our spirits were calm as we kept a watch of prayer round that little bed. The darling lay quiet and peaceful, as if she was going to take her evening sleep; her eyes, bright and very beautiful, were fixed on us; she seemed quite to know us, and sweet peace was on her dear face. She was going home – she was not to be separated from her beloved sisters. Mrs Peach sat close beside her, wetting her lips, Miss Godding on the other side. Her Father and I knelt hand in hand beside her bed; Uncle James and Aunt Lizzie at the foot of the bed. Her Father prayed with her, commended her departing soul to her dear Saviour; then I said to her the Hymn which she had chosen for her own comfort: "Away, thou dying saint, away, Flee to the mansions of the blest." I did not shrink now from saying it to her, as I had shrunk when first she asked for it. Then it had been hard indeed to say, "No more remains for thee to do," but now I knew it was well, and I turned my anguish into prayer – prayer that God would comfort us in our extreme desolation, and strengthen us to suffer and bear all His will – prayer for my Craufurd, that God would make up to him for these sweet sisters who seemed so gently leading him in the way that he should go, and that He would Himself guide him, and comfort him, and keep him from all evil influence. Yes, Craufurd; ever remember the agony of prayer for you in this sad hour. Until eight o'clock we continued thus beside her, saying texts and verses that she loved, and which she seemed to follow; and then her summons came, and the brightness of those beautiful eyes closed for ever on this world of sin and sorrow, and opened in heaven. Thus were we called upon to part with these five most blessed little daughters, each of whom had been received in prayer, and now given up, though with bitter anguish, yet with prayer and thanksgiving.'

So ended, but for yet more prayer, Catharine's narrative.

In the garden at this hard-won Hallsteads I looked about me for hope or humour, at least a perspective, a hand to hold. Suddenly it was no good consulting the look of the landscape. It lay beyond humanness, as arcane as maths: symbols of varying powers like ewe or shrub or stone inscribed at differing levels on the graph of meadows that converted to hieroglyphs of fern at the treeline – all of it presenting to the eye an insoluble problem set out in terms which themselves lay on an extreme of the borderline of comprehension. For once the sky, rising above the geometry of these peaks, looked nearer than the earth. At least heaven seemed accessible. Out of the blue I seemed much closer to something Catharine was close to.

To judge as much on likelihood as by result, the Taits tried for children in that upper room at Hallsteads. Archie hadn't it in him perhaps; or with Catharine nothing took. Their bodies froze as hard as their souls. They still had little Lucy to look after ('I then went up to nurse baby') and their grief to nourish, as well as their son racing his boyhood in fits and starts over these uneven grounds. It was to be two years before Agnes was born. Meanwhile throughout the house Walter was at work, alternating his cousin Hannah's smack of incest with Bates the parlourmaid in her pert uniform of age-old fantasy. Tired of the empty spaces of country living, this man was well and truly in rut. An afternoon was interminable without an assignation. The chasms between meals yawned for intrigue. I kept regretting without shame my slight preference, not for Catharine writing her heart out in a room with a view, but for Walter fucking his brains out in bed with his relative. ' "Make haste and go away," said she, "I am so frightened." '

I gazed into the meadow with eyes unlike my own. The bull never quite pawed the ground, but he tossed his head and charged with ineffective brevity at some illusion in the hedge. At that moment a crescendo of male shouts and female screams arose within the house and out of a number of narrow doors the students stampeded into the stableyard. It was the start of the academic day. In age most of these boys and girls were within a year or two of my children. They had the same clatter and rampancy and unfocus; they filled their space to overflowing with crass hilarity. At the back, in charge, stood and chatted the instructors, bearded chaps with big shoulders, whose authority the kids were innocuously writing off with the nudge of a joke or insult. Elsewhere, dotted about the world, consigned by their offspring to middens of amiable ill will, shrunk the parents.

Between bushes that barely hid the dustbins, I watched the future massed on the cobbles of the yard, students in groups as mettlesome as the horses that daily trotted Tait to his duties, neighing out the supremacy of the present under a clock that had stopped. They had been conceived in the unquestionability of desire, most of them wanted, all loved. At similar moments, the world over, their parents had lain in beds along and athwart the criss-cross pattern of the streets in cities or at intervals in gaps of country. They had been made out of a contortion of limbs, pillows, brains, seconds before their mother passed into dreams shared or at odds with their father, dreams down the ages under one roof, dreams in a psychic swell that overtopped frontiers and straits and mountain ranges and time zones – and slipped (invisible, silent, untouched) into nothingness; or into the archive.

Turning to the immediate view, I had expected the bull, prince of the potent, to mount at least a fantasy on my behalf. But he was a sad old party alone in a field and he just settled down to munching grass. I looked back at the facade of Hallsteads, a home to the vigorously living as much as a shrine to the so-called dead. By now the students had been hived off to seminars in converted bedrooms or ordered off to practise saving people on the mountainside. The corridors were agape, settings for dreams yet to take form. The social rooms had nobody in them but the usual spectres.

Two

The next day, as planned, O eternal God, who hast made all things for man and man for your glory, I checked our Saab in for another service at the garage outside Carlisle. The courtesy car dropped me as usual in the street by the department store alongside the cathedral. Under the Tait memorial window, from the outside a network of dark tracery invisible in detail, hosts of daffodils bloomed on a swell of lawn.

I walked under the arch to confront the old Deanery. Here for me was measured for ever the inch between life and death, exaggerated a thousandfold to the length of a cricket pitch, which divided the Tait children who were already ill in the Deanery and those isolated at No. 7 Abbey in strong hopes of survival. Waving from the windows opposite, smiling out of them, they displayed the awkward cheer of home-made art from behind the panes.

Nobody much was about today. A maid in black with a white apron carried a tray of coffee across a courtyard. Briefly she was prey for Walter. Though unusually turned off by black stockings, which stirred in him thoughts only of mourning, he made short work of servants in thrall to church or clergy. I stared at the only sound, the clack of her heels below the busy curves of leg, and could blame no one. It was as much nature for that maid to churn in a bed with Walter as to die in one before she grew old enough to be confirmed by Tait.

A verger in a plump black robe swirled out of sight. The immensity of the cathedral was void, the administration a murmur behind closed doors. In the north transept I stared upward as if in worship. The Tait girls in lamb's clothing high in the lurid window now had the sun projecting their images into the gloom within. With the best will in the world I still could not find it in my heart to think that it meant much to the here and now, even if I went on telling myself that it must. As in a dream the only contemporaneity it had was with the past. In the present the iron gates of the chapel were shut against closer scrutiny.

I turned to inspect again the Tait memorabilia. These glassed-in tatters of pain had months ago drawn me into the search now ending. Since my first look, when I last had the car serviced, certain items had been added. With a quickening of concern I saw the ten-year-old Catty's handwriting – Catharine Anna Tait inscribed on the flyleaf of a pamphlet of hymns someone had given her. Then, too tiny to be a book but thick, quite a handful for little fingers to grasp, with a lock to keep its secrets, lay a collection of poetic gems presented to the children's mother, when she too was young, by her aunt Elizabeth Spooner. From these pages the Dean's wife had read to her growing brood, and then to her diminishing one, sharing with them the visions of her own childhood versified to death.

Also new to the display was a photograph. It pictured the three daughters who evaded the month of massacre in 1856, Lucy by the luck of infancy, Edith and Agnes by being born respectively two and four years later in

London, when their father was in the thick of his episcopate. They looked unappealing, these almost adult girls, an overweight duet poised over a solo Lucy seated at the piano. Walter's unerring eye gave them no more than a second glance.

I gazed once more at the lone heights of the stained glass, really wondering why I so little wanted to examine it in detail. The semitic symbolism now repelled me as I never dared admit when a boy. Sheep in their stupidity and shepherds in their servility struck me as images of innocence too cheap for words. The brilliant clashes of colour hurt my eye as sharply as did the portraiture of saints gesturing in dumb melodrama.

Then suddenly a sound: the twiddle of a phrase broke out of the organ behind me, a brief progression ending in a trill unresolved. It shivered down my back like fear, as if the whole of the window had suddenly shattered into speech. Was the phrase a theme or not quite? Was some unseen figure on the point of improvising? Or just practising a difficult passage in a work I ought to know or starting a masterpiece from scratch? Whatever the answer, this phrase thrown out into the vault, now drifting into echo, was too good to miss, arousing boyhood in me, firing me with the old greed.

On tiptoe I walked up a side aisle into the choir. Close to the clergy's stalls, Tait's among them, complete with misericords carved under their seats into caricatures, I stood in mid-chancel staring up at display pipes as soaring as the acoustics which lent a mighty resonance alike to reedy tone of hautbois and boom of double diapason. For up there on high, in the womb of the loft, a half-unseen figure was quietly working on a performance of what was to come.

In the slanted mirror above his head, designed for keeping an eye of discipline on the now absent choir below, only his shoulders were visible. A few notes escaped his fingers as a prelude to more silence. In his pauses he added in pencil to the score a memo as to registration, a short cut to fingering, or a footnote, a guide to invention, to bypassing the obvious, a reminder of the twists and turns of the byways ahead of him, evolving into the main track of the coda that would at journey's end draw into the terminus of the last chord. It was all in the future. These were the nervous and unnerving preliminaries. In full view of the mirror he tightly wrung his hands. With an in-and-out click-clack of stops he amalgamated the tones he wanted. He fixed his choice of tempo by setting off the tick-tock of a metronome; unless he broke its rule of time he would make no music. He was at the start of life. He was at once a boy with the prospect of immortality before him and a man old enough to enjoy even the triumph of a death with which this work of his hands and mind must close.

Off the beat, against time, the organist's hands launched with bravura into the work he was tackling or extemporising. I stood entranced. I recognised authority in the roar of sound. He was putting through their paces not only the resources of this vast Harrison & Harrison instrument at Carlisle but all the music written down the European centuries to exploit its undoubted power as well as a tenderness not always accorded the organ, celebrating to the echo one composer after another, from hints of Bach's incomparably moving logic in the south of Germany through the full-blooded munificence of Parry's England to touches of

Messiaen birdsong in a French hedgerow – a mixture with additions, enriched by the odd flourish and extended by a diversion or two, all pounding into my head between snatched breaths of silence.

The pause was a long one. What would he do next? I remembered that in middle age I once attempted an act of faith. Someone told me of an organ advertised for sale in a church paper. It sat flat and untuned in the Midlands. The nonconformist chapel was going electronic. They wanted rid of the mechanics of their past. It had one manual and half a dozen stops, and in a pine case stood squat and square in the same spot for a century. A lady minister and I negotiated on the phone. We agreed on a price that undervalued both its tone and its longevity. I came, I saw, I fell for it at a glance.

With friends I hired a van. In a day we dismantled that organ, marking every pipe in chalk with a number that corresponded to its position in the soundboard. We separated wind-trunks from bellows. With care and respect we laid down the pipes as horizontal and thin as the cadavers of children on the grass outside. As, panting with effort, we moved out the body of the instrument into light that had not touched it since it was built, the chapel behind us gaped, the heart torn out. We took apart the three dimensions and entombed them prone in the back of the van and drove them a couple of hours to London in the hope that we would remember enough of their precise structure to resurrect them at home in a day or two, for preference adding dimensions as we went along.

We managed it just before our recall faded. Each screw found its socket, every pipe its place in the groove. The instrument rose again, this time to within an inch of the ceiling. We drank wine to it. We ate bread and cheese in the shadow it cast on the sitting room. The guests departed. Then alone, quaking with anxiety, I plugged my childhood love in to the domestic supply.

Playing an organ alone was still to cross a frontier between the world out there, which needed explaining, and the world in here, which was beyond explanation: the two enjoyed no colloquy. The keys were stained nicotine brown from use and age, but not such constant use as the ivories as worn as teeth on the old organ in the parish church in Hampshire which had set me off on a quest for the perfect. With elation in my bones I switched on and heard the wind swell into place.

I tried a note or two. None of the stops was full-bodied. I strained to hear sounds – reedy, stringy, diapasonic – projected in all their strength from distant memory. Nonetheless the ancient power, if weak, was here where I wanted it, under my own roof. I had brought the mystery home. It was all mine. I closed my eyes and let the hands and feet do what they wanted to touch off music: the plod of chords interrupted off and on by a scream of error, to echo life's way of improvising itself, surprising itself, criticising itself. My mind floated off as the rest of my faculties hogged a language I had never learnt to speak, but which spoke for me, if only in riddles. It was a form of half-sleep curled up in the arms of boyhood.

For I had known it from the first lurch of puberty. A compulsion in the loins was tangled not only with church attendance but with music: an alternative to the verbal, one I felt more at ease in. I knew my fingers would take off into a life of their own once I sat on an organ stool of my own.

197

That day, in middle age, the fingers had idly begun to wander. The range of stops, if limited, intoxicated me. I still had choices. This was only a start. I was recharging my age by reliving my youth. I was gaining on time. A few bars wobbled me close to self-praise. Notes clashed in dissonances that sounded new to my ears. My confidence flourished as I recalled that nobody was listening to me; I could do what I pleased. I was a free agent, making music for the spheres, extemporising life at the expense of order and discipline, against all tedium, putting prosiness to flight, dismissing every hint of the negative, accentuating the positive as loudly as possible. When I dropped my hands to the keyboard, a football crowd leapt to its feet to bellow an anthem, a packed house applauded a full orchestra at the Albert Hall, a dogfight zoomed in and out of the skies of my childhood, an express broke steaming out of a tunnel, a ship swung towards the Continent with a triumphant blast from the funnel, and all this massed music made a bid for the heavens.

At last, wrung out, I stopped, my invented self having run out of heart, my fingers aching with the trial of making it all up, my feet cramped from treading the darkness of the pedals, my ears ringing; and the silence that had been there all the time fell mercifully back into my sitting room and I fell back into myself. The bellows sighed as I turned off the wind. A sense of satisfactory inadequacy filled and fulfilled me.

In the cathedral at Carlisle I was still dithering under the arch which upheld the organ loft. A narrow stair with an even narrower door spiralled down from above. I waited a moment or two, not knowing whether I wanted to see the human face of the divine player, if I wanted to be brought back to earth or not. I had heard the whisper of the organ breathing its last, power shut off. Surely the man, whose face I had not seen even in the mirror, had to come down from the heights. The metronome had stopped ticking. He was trying to scribble down the best of what he had invented, but it was as evasive as a dream; he could know what magic he was doing only when he did it and then he was too busy doing it to know. Memory reminded him only of what he had missed. He was sitting on the stool, his hands kneading each other for comfort. All their power had seeped out.

As I waited, a pulse began droning on the air as if to fill the space left by the cut-off metronome. It sounded otherworldly. It came from the direction of the side chapel where the Tait window rose against the outer sky. On earlier visits, and indeed this morning, the wrought-iron gates of this transept had been locked fast. But with this high-powered mutter in my ear, thinking it imaginary, I rounded a pillar to find those gates wide open. On the floor grovelled a vacuum cleaner, moving in jerks sideways, as someone unseen drew on its flex. My eye followed the tube upward. On the top rung of an aluminium ladder a young man was wielding the business end, sucking the dust off the shelf under the vivid saints who enwreathed the five little girls posing as lambs. They were being cleaned, looked after, put to bed. Someone at last was attending to them, a young man in trainers and jeans, straining to reach up to their level, his dull job to make sure that no dirt or decay came between them and the present. He looked down, then up. Holding steady the long connection, which trailed in half-coils across the sanctuary, he stretched higher, only to see the lead snagged on the altar rail below. The unapplied cleaner dragged air uselessly in.

In that sacred place he uttered Walter's favourite word. Out of the shadows, by a tomb she had been dusting, came a young woman. With a flick of her wrist she released the lead, which at once looped upwards in a wriggle past the straight inscription Tait had caused to be written in stone about his fivefold loss. She was in a black skirt, echoing that earlier maid carrying the coffee. She wore black shoes and tights, a suggestion of mourning, but taking it easily, doing a job. Youth was blindly hers, so hope was too, plus despair, not to say boredom, and lots of irritation. Walter would glance at her twice, but regret the hose for lack of allure. All I thought was how close she was to the dead girls not so much in age but here and now in fact.

She sat half on her haunches, paying out the lead, supplying the electricity. At a stark angle to the ancient wall the boy stood on tiptoe, arms almost unsocketed as he reached for the uppermost dust. The T-shirt rode high up his back. The jeans tightened at his buttocks. He was doing his modern best in a setting inconceivably old. I glanced at the squatting girl, the slim boy reaching out, the ugly glamour of the past colouring that window, the present seeking a point to all the vanity. And for a second the twain met.

Three

From Cumberland the journey south to Wales was a ritual. I had performed it many times in twenty years, either spending a day amid murderous traffic to arrive at dusk or leaving late and being sure in the reverie of the night only of dimly lit landmarks. This was to be the last time, and we chose the dark.

Accompanied by a slumbrous trio, I was setting off from familiar ground, in the hope of arriving at a distant place for years identified as paradise: a literal journey shaped as distinctly as the rite of holy communion and with similar longueurs on the way. As I swung the car out on to the A7, the service entered my mind in a monotone. Our Father, which art in heaven, hallowed be thy name, we gained speed towards Longtown and soon our children in the pew behind were invading each other's space, munching sandwiches intended for hours later, give us this day our daily bread, squabbling over rights, and we were nagging them over our shoulders, deliver us from evil, Amen.

As with any ritual, I sighed with relief as each landmark passed. The M6 at Carlisle was free of traffic; we semicircled the city, its penumbra of light arching the western sky. I thought of Tait, his fond dislike of the place, reading the service to two or three gathered in his sight a mile or so from our rapid progress south. Almighty God, unto whom all hearts be open, all desires known, and from whom no secrets are hid, I did not yet know how to take your servant, Archibald Campbell Tait, into my life; though he had been for months in my heart. 'But when we moved to Carlisle,' he said, 'all was new . . . The Deanery and Cathedral were in the middle of the town, and she soon made her home a centre to which the poor looked for sympathy and help. I remember that this innovation on old prescribed ideas of Cathedral etiquette was at first not regarded with any great favour by the inhabitants of the "Abbey", as the Cathedral precincts were in Carlisle called. Yet certainly my dear wife sacrificed none of the other duties of the Deanery House to her works amongst the poor. Her poor neighbours were encouraged to come at stated times and under proper restrictions to make their wants known at the Deanery, and she went out at regular hours to visit such of them as seemed to require her presence in their homes . . .

'The chief happiness of her domestic life', he went on, 'was in the children who one after another were born to give brightness to the dingy old Deanery. Each day while we were in residence she would sally forth in our open car with the whole body of them when an interval came from the work of the day. In spring-time and in summer we would encamp some four or five miles beyond the smoke of the city, and wander with them, seeking wild-flowers in the woods or loitering pleasantly by the river-side. And then as the elder of them grew up, what pleasant hours she spent in reading with them, and how wonderfully she was able to interest their growing intelligence in all the good works which she herself did for Christ's sake. The Cathedral services, too, were both to her and to them a never-ceasing source of interest. There might be much to improve in the Cathedral – it had certainly a somewhat forlorn air when we first became acquainted with it – but to her it was ever God's House; she sought and received daily blessings from it.'

Carlisle lay far to the back of us. Rising into the lakeland heights in the dark, children sleeping behind me, I felt more than usually alert to danger, to death's close presence. My hands were clasped tightly at ten to two on the wheel, as I steered up towards Shap where lorries were blown over and the big black world shrunk under the stars. I believe in one God, the Father Almighty, maker of heaven and earth, and of all things visible and invisible, and at such moments alone at night I wished to God I did.

In the last year of the war we were all told a bishop was coming to our church. He was intending to confirm us. By placing his fingers on our heads he would admit us to the true and only faith. At personal inconvenience he was travelling from a distant city where he had his seat. The laying on of hands was a reward for our learning by heart a rigmarole of dogma that gained its power from making as much sense to a schoolboy in wartime Hampshire as to a host of Palestinians at the dawn of the epoch. The advent of the bishop posed the same type of threat as the sub-organist. He was going to put me through a secret rite.

As we boys and girls practised sitting next to one another at the communion rail, enjoying the odd nudge or relaxing into the bodily warmth, I had a worry that this ritual was about losing my virginity. Absurd: my knowledge of the phrase suggested I had already lost it dozens of times in church halls, bell towers, vestries, organ lofts, vicarages. This unique procedure at the altar was in theory to gain me something far above that loss: a blessing that lay beyond understanding, until bread became flesh in my mouth washed down by blood in the form of wine. I expected a very torrent of metaphor as the first wafer blotted my tongue and too little blood was trickled down my throat.

We kneeled, close up. I was next to the girl who had put me on a pony and led me to that chapel with the dud harmonium. The sub-organist was at the organ. His fluty music mooned with sentiment. I leant against her, loins tingling. Down the line the bishop was two or three candidates away from us, muttering whatever mantra drew children at a stroke into maturity. She put her folded hands down between her thighs half-open under the skirt and sighed desirously in readiness for her blessing. Straining nylon encased knees that shone. Almighty God, maker of all things, judge of all men, my trousers reared enough to oblige me for comfort to bend deeply forward over the rail at just the moment of the bishop's hand reaching out to me. Neck cricked, I looked up at his glazed eye. And I saw someone who knew next to nothing of the nature of faith. His inner glance projected a blankness almost professional. His fingers briefly caressed my head. Beside me the girl's knuckles contorted on her knee as jerkily as a crab. My hair ruffled by the episcopal touch, I entered the fraternity of the church with an erection in which brother Walter would have taken due pride. But it all led for the moment to nothing. There was a cream tea afterwards at which girls and boys were segregated as though the effect of confirmation was to arouse guilt. We sat on different sides of the room staring at one another in the hostile mirror of sex.

Lulled by the murmur of the engine past Lancaster, I thought back to the day's imponderables. Here I was, looking forward to sleep two hundred miles away, asking what contribution would today's events make to tonight's dreams? Maybe none: the present often delayed its glide into a dream, to put me off the scent. I might wait weeks for this afternoon's input – or, if I survived, as many years – to be converted into archive material. Time, as the clock on the dashboard understood it, had nothing to do with the process. At great speed a parallel train rattled its lights past us on the way to Euston. Walter was locked into seduction somewhere aboard; thou shalt not commit adultery. Lord, have mercy upon us, and incline our hearts to keep this law. Signs to places unvisited flashed past, Blackburn, Liverpool, Manchester, all bishoprics Queen Victoria in her pity set aside, even if they existed, when translating Tait to the greater diocese of London.

A sense of the timeless crept into the car's roll through the dark. The others were asleep. A few sighs, a snore at intervals. I wondered again whether dreams were meant as messages or merely gave the hint of a significance to our limited brains for the purpose of putting us off any scent at all. It struck me as possible, regarding God as I did in boyhood – God who being so secretive must know best, God whose cruelties must conceal a divine plan which not even the enlightened could decode – that dreams resorted to similar stratagems of privacy, to keep us at bay, to stop us knowing too much while maintaining our curiosity, to retain our respect by holding us awestruck. Tait bore all that out. So did Catharine in her sturdy faith.

For years this drive into the Welsh night had occupied the back of my mind as a species of dream. The eyes were rapt by the road, as goggled as in death. The brain was released from thought into images. I had long considered going to bed as going to work, viewing the point of my existence as part of the action of a story that took place only at night. I lost sight of, or swiftly forgot, the day's chores, as dreams got busy transmitting a selection of them to a level – as in a car at night, as at a holy mass – at once permanent and outside time. We were all factories, daily mining the raw material that got processed in the dark behind closed doors. Our sleep was the most creative third of our day. We were making things of vital use out of substances that were immaterial. At the last, having thereby made a unique contribution to something beyond us, each of us was to die into that insubstantial but immortal nowhere. Eternity might well be a man perpetually drowning in craftier, funnier, superior versions of his own memories. Eternity might turn out to be breathlessly nice.

At the difficult turn-off of the M62 into Wales, I recalled how I dropped into this depth of interest in dreams. It occurred in a smart street in London a quarter of a century ago. I had to spell out that affair now and again; dreamlike it too was apt to fade, if only on grounds of improbability. Living at a high pitch of an urban spring in a haze of romance, I was thrilled body and soul by this woman whose roots were everywhere, America, Europe, Israel. I was all set for the revelatory. In her house tucked away south of Hyde Park I woke up in the small hours, a dream rapidly fading, catching hold of its tail, with a sure punch of knowledge, which annoyingly made it fade faster, that the dream had in fact been taking place not just in my mind, but hers.

Out of her mouth, close to mine, came a whimper. A whimper was just what a second earlier I had emitted, a sound synchronous enough to have started me awake. A glimmer of light angled across the bed from the street. Dozens of people were sleeping closely to us as we lay in the slack of love letting our mental innards mull over the aftermath. I felt her damp thigh slung over my hip as surely as I knew that our heads were engaged in a conspiracy. We were serving that conspiracy without being aware of its presence, let alone its point. I was half asleep, she wholly. The amazement thrilled me like an uprush of desire. My groin stirred. I could not bear to wake her. I had to, I dared not, and then in a miracle of timing, as I thought it, her eyes rolled open on the darkness, rather with bewilderment than affection, and she murmured with clarity half a phrase, which sprang absolutely out of the dream, at least as I was now hanging on to the last misty drift of it, and then almost in a flounce she turned over, thrusting her bottom at me, sinking into the pillow, as if determined to renew the dream and keep the rest of it to herself. She little guessed as yet that a force beyond herself was already at work to steal it.

I knew at once that I would meet this delicious being in another sphere. I had just to fall back to sleep to join her wherever she was. My eyes were stuck wide. I was worried I might forget this whole waking episode as if it were a dream and be unable to tell her in the morning, and then as the shaft from the street lamp fell athwart our bed as if time were immobilised, I knew that it all mattered enough never to be forgotten. I ran my fingers down the curve of her prone spine, shaped a buttock with my hand, and slipped into oblivion at the last minute wondering whether or where I would be joining her. It felt as I sank like the most popular form of death ever adumbrated. Let your light so shine before men, that they may see your good works, said I.

For mile after mile of the communion service, extending halfway down England and across much of Wales, nobody in the car woke up. There was a motorway stop, everyone still half asleep. My son ran off to pee. In the shop he grabbed more sandwiches to replace those he had eaten too early on the journey. We do not presume to come to this thy table, O merciful Lord, trusting in our own righteousness, but in thy manifold and great mercies. The drone of lorries grinding past sounded as deep as a pedal note long sustained. Below the arch of stars the air of the night smelt tainted by fuel. Our bent-headed stance at the urinals was to bow in respect at an altar. He raced to the machine arcade; just slip money into the slot of the offertory, and you were at once connected to a higher force. We took our pews again in church and drove back on to the motorway.

We were not worthy so much as to gather up the crumbs under thy table, but my secret was a pheasant sandwich in greaseproof and a half-finished bottle of claret saved from a shooting lunch. I steered on. My wife moaned in sleep beside me, as we entered the dreams of Housman country somewhere south of Wrexham. The boy, kicked into wakefulness by tuna mayonnaise, writhed on the back seat as disturbingly as a conscience.

My thoughts preyed on that forthcoming sandwich and the wine to wash it down. Meanwhile we were slipping unnoticed into the nineteenth century at Llandrindod Wells, where neither the Taits took the waters nor Walter the maidservants. I was on my way to closing down my life so as presumably to open it up. Along the valley the street lamps flickered in strings of candles as I rushed past, and then we were into the jet secrecy of the hills. All seemed quiet at my rear, evermore praising thee and saying holy, holy, holy, as I extricated the sandwich from its wrapping, and driving this last lap with one hand got its gamey edge to my mouth. I bit into the good bread. Grant us therefore, gracious Lord, so to eat the flesh of thy dear Son Jesus Christ, and to drink his blood, that our sinful bodies may be made clean by his body. Fumbling into the plastic bag on the floor near the gears, I thumbed the cork off the Léoville-Barton '89 and, eyes ogling the road, took a good swig or two, our souls washed by his most precious blood. In memory a flick of lace wiped the chalice clean, that we may evermore dwell in him, and he in us.

We were nearing home. There was only a spell of mountainous darkness to switchback through. I again let my soul feel washed by guzzling, round a hairpin bend, the dregs of the claret. Soon we were free-wheeling downhill towards the home which tomorrow we would no longer own, as disconcertingly as if we were all leaving one another, father, mother, daughter, son, a domestic diaspora not a soul wanted, just because of the practical need to quit an object as tame as a house where we had all grown up together. The Taits were never so sentimental or self-pitying as this, our Father.

They showed strength which art in heaven. They got on with life, hallowed be thy name.

In the smallest of the small hours, dead beat, we bumped up the lane to the invisible paradise that was already no more ours as of noon.

Four

They all flopped into bed, the family. I looked at them wakefully. Driving had left me sleepless. Their faces sweetened. Dreams were on the way. They slept within the fragile present of their rooms. Books tomorrow to be disrupted lined the passages. Walls were shadowy with images that timed their growing up. Hung on hooks or bedposts were the dolls or animals they had clung to. Time was rushing out. I had only one night, and I dreamed it out as the moon waned, forgetting it all instantly. Leaving this world in Wales was a rehearsal for dying. Meanwhile the Taits were moving out of the Carlisle Deanery.

The men came early. The high vans dwarfed the house. They packed at speed. My son digging out his own detritus in the roof found a redstart's corpse. Fragments of old journeys – boarding cards, restaurant bills, train tickets, timetables – got tossed on to a fire in the yard. Out of the smoke memoranda fluttered into oblivion. A pyre of souvenirs briefly clouded a pure blue day. Without a sound an awakened owl flew to and fro under the roof of the barn as we cleared it. By now the Taits were packing up at London House in St James's Square. A last jug of our white buddleia stood on the bookcase which within an hour was lying flat on its back in the van. We all ate lunch standing, plates balanced on piles of linen, in a mood slightly hysterical, almost of relief, fatigue all round. Catharine was ahead of us, supervising the placement of her things in Fulham Palace.

Meanwhile the movers pursued their paid act of destruction. Their job was to make the place vanish before our eyes into thin air. I could only watch and make tea for them until they conjured the kettle into a packing case. The heat of the day grew to a zenith that dripped sweat. Every bedroom was soon voided into a cavern awaiting a new furniture of birth, love, death. In London, well in advance by now, Catharine was choosing familiar pieces, on Archie's accession to the throne of Canterbury, to make Addington a home for him. Our kitchen was being drained of its meals and stripped of its memories. As the body of our belongings was at last borne off, the spirit fled it. The sun was going down. I detected and detested what passed through the mind, sidelong or with a stab, when the end was in sight: the false comforts, the brain's last-minute bid for a belief in an afterlife, the regrets for things not done rather than for things done or done improperly, the hasty awkward preparation for becoming extinct tomorrow, the last look at the scene around you, the view blurred by a tear, an effort at a wry smile to keep you in humour, a race against time to remember all that ever happened to you unless you knew you had already put it on permanent record in dreams slipped into the archive, and fatalism, and defiance, if you dared, O Lord God, in whom we live, and move, and have our being.

As the Taits in mournful triumph were moving into Lambeth Palace, we drove back with exhaustion to the Kennington Road.

Five

I had put off the pilgrimage to Canterbury long enough. The Son of God's first stronghold in my homeland, this city had to be the terminus of the search for what was left of him or of Tait or of me for that matter. Here was a dead end to force me to a conclusion. There I should kneel, receive the ritual of a blessing, and go home, wherever home was to be. There also Tait had ended up in marmoreal absence; his body lay elsewhere.

The day chosen was Palm Sunday. When in error my diary had got stuffed into the packing-up of our place in Wales, the year dissolved into oblivion. I had no idea what appointments I had in the future, if any. I lacked means of checking what had occurred in the past. My real life mixed bizarrely with my true one. Lunches at my club with Archie Tait became confused with the funeral of a close friend. I wondered on which date precisely I had spent a weekend in Carlisle and awoken from dreams in the small hours to the tread of illicit feet, and envied Walter as much his luck as his lust. The loss of this diary was like burying an old friend, an essential part of oneself. Time past and time future were both wiped out at the whim of a packer I had later overtipped.

Meanwhile in storage the mice were nibbling into my year. A spreading damp was blotting out the nights when in St James's Square I crept to the side of Catharine's bed for help or innocently went to the movies in the Haymarket in the vicinity of the Argyll Rooms where Walter strutted in quest of stimulus. Imported into the warmth of the diary from the cold house in Wales, insects had nested and reproduced, eating up records of many a good night's sleep peopled by dreams gone for ever, either nowhere or into the higher record. I looked forward to the grim pleasure of fetching out my past in tatters, with all those blank days, when trying to reconstruct from a deficient memory events that had no significance. It would be as hopeless an exercise as if I had dreamed them in the first place. But in theory I would get my life back when it all came out of store.

On that first day in Carlisle I had seen Tait's plaster maquette a foot long in the showcase. Now I was ready to view him lifesize in the permanence of stone. Palm Sunday: the time of year of Chaucer's *Prologue*, sweet showers piercing last month's drought, and gangs of anorak pilgrims from all over the globe moving idly around the close: it was forbidden on a Sunday morning to enter the cathedral except for worship. The building outside stood in soaring order. Inside was as deep as the grave it was. The morning sent down thin patterns of sun through the tracery. A few faces were laced by light. In the choir the service was austere, a brief version of matins for Lent without a note of music.

What had been done?

A journey of mine had examined a faith that sustained a family through a domestic disaster that would floor most of us. This documentary had shown how hard I found it, at any age since boyhood, to embrace a faith, either a universal one, such as just being human, or one of my own devising.

What had been done? During the trip – at that pub in Addington with Tait standing high in the window of the church next door, on the Carlisle train with Catharine opposite me facing the engine, in spare moments at our haunted houses near Llandovery or in Lambeth round the block from Tait's palace – I had taken notes. These notes were meant to cast light on the true nature of faith, only to have that light refracted at an invisible angle by the very nature of my demand. On later reading these notes made no sense: they stuck at framing the questions, let alone blurting the answers. All my work was in the margins.

I had no idea where in the cathedral, this store of saints and martyrs, Tait was to be found. The steps to Becket's appointment with death, or rather his shrine, were worn hollow by centuries of credulous knees. But where was Archie's memorial? The service ended, and help was to hand. A lady verger, taking my prayer book and letting me keep my palm crucifix, asked me to wait while she ushered out the laggardly. She was handsome in robes. With a touch of Walter's impertinence I felt the lure of her piety. Her job done, she opened a wrought-iron gate in a side aisle. She smiled. A few yards on, and she lifted the plush sling of another barrier. She bowed. I passed under. Showing me with a degree of ceremony into not a bedroom but the north-east transept, she asked in a whisper whether I minded if she left me to it. I shook my head in wonder. Her footsteps diminished nimbly elsewhere. My vestige of Walter never saw her again.

I had the whole cathedral around me, and above me, and on my side, and under me. Nobody was present. The organist had not been called to duty. Priests had hastened off to late breakfast or early sherry. The shiver of the absence of God was mine alone, as was the usual kick from the invisible man at my back. The light darkened from clouds passing beyond the plain glass in the arches above. The one illumination was the white of the tomb.

Archibald Campbell Tait was a blanched figure in marble lying on his back. He represented the image of an archbishop laid to rest in the more feminine of his official finery. Beneath this perpetual lying-in-state his mortal body, as often impassioned in life as it was wrung by grief, did not putrefy, mummify, or even exist. So convincing was the presence that I kept having to remember that he was actually buried in the modesty of Surrey next to his wife and son; his elegy in a country churchyard lay in the suburbs of Croydon. If the Queen had decreed his memorial to lie heavily here in Canterbury at the heart of church and state, the lighter whereabouts of his spirit had been his own choice. Under Addington he lay in bed with Catharine as his bones were stripped of flesh and duly joined hers in the amity of corruption.

On one flank of the white sepulchre were inscribed Archie's names and dates. On the opposite side a tribute to a man wholly without fault was chiselled. These were words, had you been following his career, were you in love with him, if you admired what he had suffered or took heart from his life's ministry or message, to bring tears sheeting down your face. There was the pleasure of Tait's having existed enough to give you reason to question existence. There was, too, his valuing lots of existence despite unholy amounts of pain.

He lay there somewhat at peace, fixed for ever. His face was drawn into gloom by the sculptor's assertion of his subject's faith. Back into my mind swam his thirties as headmaster of Rugby in all their fatigue: that drowsiness which he thought a fault he had to conquer, but turned out to be rheumatic fever, weakening for good his lungs and heart – Catharine had summoned his family to take leave of him. In his fifties his face seized up, his arm paralysed never to be unnumbed – Catharine that night wrote to his sister that the family was 'simply waiting for the end'. But six more years slipped by before on Ash Wednesday 1875 he wrote, 'This day has of old been a solemn day to me. Twenty-eight years have passed since the doctor came to my bedside at Rugby and told me how I must expect to die.' And seven years later still he was adding with relief, 'I have been thinking today of the deaths of all my intimate friends. Few have passed through it without long and painful struggle. It is well there is One who invites us to cast all our care upon Him.'

In effigy Tait looked by no means carefree. But he had survived, for longer than he dared hope, the things he termed the 'trials, privileges, opportunities' of his time. His face had immediacy. He had the air of an intellectual enjoying a poor night's sleep. He lay on his back as though waiting for Catharine to kneel gently over him and disarrange his robes. The features retained in age, for eternity, his slightly butch look of sensitive sexiness. For a second I wondered where on earth Walter was entombed.

Tait's attitude was a touch critical of the sculptor Boehm, who had nonetheless had the last word. The slippers were immaculately carved, as further on were the vestments. Had Tait been standing up, they were hanging in the right folds. But the stony lengths of hair that lay in bangs around the ears reduced his dignity, even if their cut brought the old fellow back into more recent fashion. Only then, thinking his face slightly petulant and not at all at rest, did I observe that he had dirty ears. These ears, if finely shaped by both his maker and the mason, had accumulations of grime in them. Over the century since piety established him in this transept, the cathedral by slow degrees had gathered its comment on his unassailable purity and let it fall in a grubby manna from on high.

Not far distant stood the massive rear of the organ. Manly harmonies of huge Victorian compass and volume surely marked the ceremony when Tait's tomb was unveiled. The rafters, or rather the vault, must have rung. In the decades that followed, every part of the organ's structure – the wooden insides that footed the pipes, the bellows that creaked out dust at every blast of a trumpet – had been racked by many an act of mourning, celebrations of a victory of arms, a wedding to gladden the nation's heart: great occasions that required every stop to be pulled out, not to mention the dust if not ashes that imperceptibly fell from the shaken depths of the instrument when funeral music rumbled deep within. I now knew what had dropped tiny deposits of black grit into Tait's auricles, not with a view to discrediting a man who had listened to the smallest voice or least word, but as an unobtrusive sign of power – a footnote on the decay of all things, even things above your head. It was, of course, the organ.

Under the blank unease of Tait's body ran the epitaph. At the end of this search, which had kept me eager and unsure of myself and as truthful as I could manage, it hardly bore reading. Each line wore black. The layout challenged punctuation. The capitals shouted. It said as follows: 'A GREAT ARCHBISHOP/JUST, DISCERNING, DIGNIFIED, STATESMANLIKE/ WISE TO KNOW THE TIME AND RESOLUTE TO REDEEM IT./HE HAD ONE AIM:/TO MAKE THE CHURCH OF ENGLAND MORE AND MORE/THE CHURCH OF THE PEOPLE:/ DRAWING TOWARDS IT BOTH BY WORD AND GOOD EXAMPLE/ALL WHO LOVE THINGS TRUE AND PURE/BEAUTIFUL AND OF GOOD REPORT.'

The greatness of eternity in comparison to time came fully over me. So said Catharine close to one daughter's death. So thought I. From Hallsteads, I recalled, she wrote to a relative who had asked to read her narrative, 'Yes, you shall see it. I hope it will tell you much of God's dealings with us, and picture to you that little company of angels, first as they brightened our home on earth, and then as they left us one by one for their home in heaven. Think of them as their Father ever pictures them – as a bright chain to draw our spirits up to heaven . . .'

I backed away, almost stumbling over the plush rope in anxiety to escape this populous solitude, looking all round for the wrought-iron gates, which at last let me out near a pulpit too modern to have carried Tait's message. It stood high enough to command huge congregations. The world had to listen. A while ago nothing had stopped me stepping up, fearful of discovery, nerves shrivelling, into the tiny Jacobean pulpit which Tait occupied at Marsh Baldon during his curacy from Oxford. There and then he spoke truth as he knew it. Now I stood in the superhuman space of this taller and unique church, making no apology within for the peroration that stirred in me, wanting to project it afar, knowing quiet talk was more persuasive to most, equally knowing that the cathedral was mine alone and no one would hear me. I stood at the bottom step wondering whether to wind my way up. In a church of my own for an instant I had no call to hold myself in. From the heights of this pulpit I might inform nobody except the immortal, the invisible, how fulfilled my questioning of the Taits had enabled me to be, how little I sought answers to be handed down in my own flawed language, how thus so vibrant I was with life in any definition you chose, Almighty God, Father of all mercies, how indeed with such an unchic influx of piety and honour both the Taits had given me their lives to share.

But I failed to put my foot even on the first step up. The continuing problem I had, whenever I stumbled into saying things that sounded as stony as sermons, was how to convey silence without using words, how to make music in a speech that lent itself only to making sense, how to communicate with as many people as possible by saying as little as I could, how to create belief without sowing doubts, and whether any of these endeavours, or indeed any other effort to ease life, could any longer be thought to have any force or use. I had set about these adventures with intent to take a plunge and I had almost foundered. Not quite, though.

The Taits were still alive. I was in bed with Catharine without betraying Archie. I could wrestle with Walter's spirit in that tower study in Carlisle or collude with his chasing the housemaids at Hallsteads or rage down the Haymarket in protest against his abuse of sluttish virgins. I had saved for a more grown-up posterity the dead daughters, each of whom I identified as, or with, my own. Their dreams had entered into mine, which meant that they were alive. That quintet of girls was passing on the baton to the future. The relay of dreams would go on for good. At any time someone alive would be bearing their archive in mind. So faith – taking a jump, risking a fall – was worth a try, more gripping than boredom, art, anxiety, disillusion, political certitude, a day's work, drink, or simply living in your skin. I knew that well into the future the Taits were safe with me. And so was I with them.

At no time did I mistake my view of dreams for a stab at the literal truth. It was a metaphor that stood in for faith, while I was busy unearthing the real thing; but metaphors were real too. Any dream I had was even harder for my brain to invent than my mind to memorise. It daily dramatised my day's trivia, only to fade into a nowhere. A word like dimension missed that nowhere by a mile. Nobody had an idea of its distance from a dimension. When, where, who, why: these were the non-questions that lay as hugely beyond asking as a light-year. It was this wholesale incomprehensibility that shook me awake to the *bona fides* of faith. It shook me as profoundly, in as religious a way, as a simple belief in God or gods would stir, or might, or had stirred, someone else, millions of dead others, in Athens or Stockholm, at a variety of times, on Calvary, in St John the Divine at Kennington, here and now at Canterbury. At its extreme of intensity the sex urge never could or would or should rise to that pitch, cross that border, however Walter vaunted its power and his potency. 'I have no sense of time, all is oblivion and elysium,' said Walter.

So I had come to believe, if not wholly, in belief. I knew something of its nature and savoured all its desirability. The thinnest of membranes, if an opaque one, divided me from the reality of belief, but at least I knew that it was real. I was aware too that to think of strongly held belief as nothing but self-delusion was to evade the point. Rather was it a heartfelt and heartening way of putting a brave face on this world's inadequacies. I also believed by now that doubt was shockingly positive. It fed and fired me; it was the force that made me explore. Doubt had always been an enemy which I could now turn into a friend and make it work at faith. It would not cheat me or let me be cheated or permit me to cheat myself.

In the end it might prove to be no good pretending: I held no faith, not even as a more vital version (as preached earlier) of succumbing to the tyranny of drink, tobacco, sex, money, or any of the satraps of illusion by which, to stay nice and sane, we were obliged to live. I stood, as stated, a man never raped by experience or traumatised, but disappointed in it, forever on the brink of gloom but never quite making it to depression, almost envious of those more hurt by life than myself and thus ennobled. I was swayed by an emotion just as superstitious as faith: the bad things never happened to me because I stood out of the way of them, never took the chances, always sidestepped the blunders. I had led a cowardly life in which things either large or great failed to strike. 'Often at night, when I had hung over each little bed,' said Catharine, 'I used to feel this is too much for earth . . . It is only when we feel the nothingness of earth that we begin to know the joy we have as Christians.'

A modest faith in oneself might be an offshoot of the search. From the outset I had been seeking ways of luring my brain onward, tricking my training, making my childhood work for its keep, bringing adolescence to heel, outflanking the defences I built up as an adult, giving my inevitable complacency at seventy a nasty turn or two. I was nagging at the principle that none of us wanted to be what we thought we were. Daily the self left a sour aftertaste; much of life was hangover from over-indulgence in ego. So I had gone off on a search for methods of taking myself offguard. I had no wish to end up realising – or, worse, not noticing – that I was a mass of cliches stiffening dangerously into a platitude walking with a stick.

I noted only now that the entrance to the pulpit was locked. I gazed back at Tait's oblong of marble luminous in the gothic grey of the transept. Still nobody was occupying these acres of past; the tourists were as yet unadmitted to the cathedral. Faith had switched off the last two millennia until the hour of the next divine service. I thought back to that testimonial on the tomb and tears pricked my eyes. Archie was hardly disappointed in what the world had made of his ministry. Catharine approved of the wording, but in her breast wanted more for him. The chiselled script needed to be read to the accompaniment of a Bach fugue, if only someone were playing one, a sub-organist practising up in the loft in the lull between services, making sure he got every note right, a man from my boyhood who was not just doing it for his own pleasure, letting praise burst out of the heart of the instrument at the bid of his fingers and feet, but because he recognised a higher calling to speak in the right language about someone greater than himself.

Uncertain which exit might be available in this shut-up church, I drifted all the way down the nave past the empty seats that had patiently listened to my sermon and at length came across a side door that led out into the secular disorder of the open air, and in the burst of light outside I saw that I had reached the end of the story. The story said that nothing for seventy years had done me any harm; if hurt at all, I had now digested or dismissed the pain. I had asked my questions of life in so firm a way as to finish up not minding if I had no firm answers to them. I was no longer enslaved by the invisible, but enriched by it, in particular if and when I had contributed to it by dreaming. I had fought out a working arrangement with sex in what had often seemed its winning battle with the spirit. I had spent time as companion to two people, these nineteenth-century Taits, whom I had come to love in their own time and terms, as well as in mine. Thanks to them and their loss I had got back in touch with things in my childhood that might in age have dried into bitterness. The search had been a reminder of the finer things I had to live for during the remainder of my life. Not a step of the way had been attended by angst or hollowed by tedium or taken for granted. If the happiness I found in exploring turned out to be delusive, at the very least it was (famous last word) happiness.